THE SIGNAL SERIES

SIGNAL 41

SAVING CARSON

LC TAYLOR

Signal 41: Saving Carson
©2019 by LC Taylor
All Rights Reserved

Cover designed by Rebeca Covers
Edited by Alice I. Lunsford
Cover Model Chad Criss

LC Taylor
Visit my website
www.authorlctaylor.com

Printed in the United States of America

First Printing
Oct 2019

THANK YOU FOR DOWNLOADING SIGNAL 41: SAVING CARSON. This is the first book in the SIGNAL SERIES. Each book will be a standalone story that highlights love blooming from tragedy. All books will have a HEA with no cliff hangers.

I would like to give special thanks to several people who made this book happen. First, my husband - who sat in IHOP over breakfast, and carved out the series with me, and LeeAnn – my own personal cheerleader. Having them to bounce ideas off allows me to create something I hope everyone will enjoy. It was my husband who gave me the inspiration to use REAL MEN and WOMEN in public safety on the covers (not just a cover model).

That leads me to the third person. Chad Criss – without your smoking hot body, Signal 41 would be just another book cover. Thank you for being such a good sport and allowing me to take pictures of you in your work gear. You brought this book to life!

I would like to give a special shout out to my work-wife (you know who you are), thank you for giving up your Saturday morning to take pictures of Chad - I know it was a real burden for you.

And thank you to all my readers! Without you, I'd be writing in vain... I hope you enjoy this story. I know I had a blast writing it!

SOMETIMES PEOPLE ARE AFRAID OF FALLING IN LOVE BECAUSE IT SOMETIMES COMES IN A WAY WE NEVER EXPECTED"
TERRY MARK

As Carson sat at her kitchen table, she stared at her husband of ten years. He wasn't the same man she'd married her senior year of college. No, he'd become someone different. She supposed she had too – isn't that what happens as one gets older? People change, they grow up. Well, most people. But not him, not Phillip – at least not in the way a person should. Carson could hear him talking, the words spilling from his mouth as he screamed at her... again.

She was tired.

Tired of this life.

Tired of being alone.

But most of all, tired of his lies.

"Do you hear me, Carson?" He smacked her glass from the table, "I asked you who told you those lies."

"Lies?" Carson scoffed, "Really, with that in front of you," she tossed the cell phone bill at him, "tell me why you would have so many calls and text messages to her?"

Phillip stood, "She's my secretary – there are bound to be calls between us."

"Do you hear yourself?"

"What I hear is my ungrateful wife accusing me of something that's bullshit."

"Bullshit? BULLSHIT? Let me see your phone then," Carson stood and grabbed for his phone. But Phillip was quicker and snatched it out of her grasp.

"What the fuck is your problem?" Phillip shoved his chair back, the legs scraping the floor. "You're out of your mind."

Carson held her finger up, silencing his words, "Yeah... that's what I hoped – but then Cassie, your paralegal, saw you with her in your office. Her legs spread wide while you fucked her on your desk." Carson watched as a myriad of emotions cross his face, "so, if you still want to tell me I'm the one who is crazy, go ahead."

Phillip stood frozen in his spot. His eyes never left hers. Snapping from his trance, he turned on his heel, leaving her to watch his back as he retreated from the kitchen. "Where do you think you're going? We aren't done you son of a bitch."

"I'll be back later."

Carson stared at the large oak door as he slammed it behind him. The grain of the wood mesmerizing her. Blinking back tears, she noted the time on the clock, 1:15. She still had a little time before she needed to pick Max up at school. Grabbing her cell phone, she googled attorneys. There was no way she was staying trapped in this marriage another minute. Max would be better off with divorced parents, rather than two parents that fought non-stop. She wanted him to grow up happy and well adjusted.

After several phone calls and nearly forty minutes later, she'd secured an appointment for tomorrow, with a female divorce attorney. This had been a long time coming – it just took a woman she barely knew, to make her see what her marriage really was – a joke.

Carson gathered her purse, keys, and phone, and headed towards the school. She always picked Max up from car riders. Not working left her plenty of time to focus on him. Pulling into the school's car line, she relaxed and waited. Reading her phone to kill time, she tried to push out the thought of Phillip and Diane's affair. A whole year he'd been unfaithful. Not like it mattered, she and Phillip hadn't been intimate in over three. He probably had other women before Diane. Honestly, when Carson thought about Phillip, she knew deep down the only reason she'd married him was because she'd gotten pregnant with Max her senior year. Barely twenty-one, she found herself at the justice of the peace saying I do. The first seven years, their marriage was good – mostly. But then the late nights and drinks with friends became more and more common. Glancing up, Carson realized the line had started to move forward. Easing her car up, she didn't see Max anywhere. Unrolling her window, she asked one of the teachers if she could see where he was.

"Mrs. Harding, the front office says your husband checked him out an hour ago."

"Oh," dread filled her chest, "We must have crossed wires today. Thanks. See you tomorrow."

Carson navigated her car from the school parking lot, her stomach in knots. She knew Phillip had left on his bike, meaning her son was on the back of said bike. Another thing they fought about constantly. Rushing back home, Carson was disappointed when she pulled into an empty driveway. Where the fuck was Phillip, with her son no less?

Smacking her hands on the steering wheel, she pushed herself out and slammed the car door. She snatched her phone from her purse and immediately tried calling Phillip. Voice mail... Of course. She wanted to scream. Instead, she ran inside to wait. Hopefully, Phillip would come home so they could sit down and discuss things – without yelling.

Slow days like this one nearly killed Jason. He lived for the thrill, the rush of a call – but so far, his twenty-four-hour shift had been nothing more than keys locked in a car and hydrant duty. Being on the special operations truck, aka, squad, he typically sat around waiting for a massive fire or accident. When the bell finally went off, two hours before his shift was supposed to end, he sighed. Sitting around for almost twenty-two hours, some of which he slept, a call this close to shift change was not welcomed, it was nearly four – another two hours, and he'd be off.

Signal 41 – possible injuries.

Truck versus motorcycle.

Squad 6, Truck 6, Medic 6 respond to 7th and Main.

Jason winced. A motorcycle versus a truck never ended well. Someone usually lost a limb or their life – and it was almost always the motorcycle rider. Pulling on his turnout pants and jacket, he climbed into the passenger seat of the squad truck. His partner, Davey Stone, or Stoner as everyone called him, hoped in the driver seat. Henry Jones was third man on squad, he poured into the back seat just as Henry was rolling out the front doors.

"Maybe it won't be a bad one. Sometimes bikers just lay their bikes down in the dirt to avoid a car or truck," Henry called out from the back seat as they neared the scene.

"I hope so. I don't want to be stuck here all damn day." Davey laughed as he pulled the truck to a stop. The scene told us this was not going to be a quick one. The motorcycle laid on its side, crumpled beneath the front end of a semi-truck. The rider was on his back a few feet from the downed bike. As usual, the truck owner was standing off to the side on the shoulder of the road.

"Sir, can you tell me what happened?" Jason surveyed the scene. No jaws would be needed since the motorcycle rider was not pinned under the truck like the bike.

"I didn't see him. He just pulled out in front of me before I could react and stop, I hit him." The driver of the truck was starting to lose it.

"Sir. Why don't you go over there and let the medics look at you? I think you're going into shock."

He nodded and headed towards the awaiting paramedics. Jason surveyed the scene. A man was being restrained by officers, screaming at them. Walking towards them, Jason looked him over.

"What's going on?" The man had a gash down his leg and road rash on his forearms.

"This guy took a pretty hard hit – he's not making any sense." The officer on the scene stated.

"Sir," Jason waved his fingers in front of the man's eyes, "Can you tell me your name?"

"Phillip – and I'm fine. Please, you have to find my son."

"Were you involved in this accident?" Jason's hair stood, unease settling in his gut.

"Yes... my son and I were on my bike. I wasn't paying attention and – FUCK!"

The realization there was another person on the bike sparked Jason into action. Gripping his radio in hand, "Squad 6 all units," he took a breath, "we have another victim," releasing the mic radio, "How old is your son?"

"Seven...Oh, God, MAX?" Phillip collapsed to the ground, the medics rushed to his side.

"All units, a seven-year-old boy was on the back of the bike. Search the area." He turned, scanning the surroundings, he started towards a ditch opposite the accident scene. The kid had likely been thrown, projecting him anywhere. As he neared the edge, he caught sight of small shoes, attached to legs. Picking up his speed, he dropped to his knees next to the boy. Feeling for a pulse, he sensed it was weak.

"MEDIC!" he screamed, "I've got him!"

Paramedics swarmed, taking control of the small lifeless boy. He was in awful shape, bones protruding from both legs, his forearm bent at an odd angle, and the most concerning, his helmet laid on the ground a few feet from him. Jason snatched it up, fury filling his blood. It was an adult helmet, much too large for a small child.

He watched in anger as they loaded him and the father inside the ambulance and tore away from the accident. Jason knew there was little chance the boy would survive something like this – he wondered where the mother was. Shaking his head, he headed back to the crumpled bike. The truck driver sat on the ground, crying.

"Sir, you should go to the hospital and let them check you out."

"No – I barely felt a bump. I...Oh God, I killed a child." His sobs echoed through the air.

"No – you didn't. That kid should have never been on the back of a motorcycle. And his dad admitted to not looking before he pulled out. It's tragic – but you're not to blame. Can I call someone for you?"

The man nodded, giving Jason the phone number to his wife. As he helped clean the scene, he couldn't help but wonder about the boy. As they pulled into the station, he glanced at his watch. Their shift had been over an hour ago. Stripping his turnout gear, he headed for the locker room.

"You alright?" Mike asked.

"Just thinking about that kid – it's fucked up. You know he was wearing an adult helmet?"

"No, shit? Any reasonable rider knows your helmet has to be the right fit – it's your head you're protecting. That's fucked up – he might have had a chance if he was wearing the right size."

"Yeah. I know. Heard anything about his condition?"

"Nah – you know we rarely find out the outcome of a call." Mike studied Jason, "Go to the hospital – find out. You're going to let this eat at you until you get closure. But Jason," Mike rested his hand on Jason's shoulder, "you need to know it's not going to be good."

He nodded, grabbing his backpack, and headed out. It felt wrong to take his bike to the hospital, a machine like this destroyed a family. Regardless, he needed to know if the boy had any chance.

Carson paced in her kitchen as she waited. It was nearly six and she'd still not heard from Phillip. She was getting ready to call him when her cell phone flashed an unknown number.

"Hello?"

"Is this Mrs. Harding?"

"Yes," her tone filled with irritation, "This is Carson Harding."

"Mrs. Harding, this is officer Browning with the Carver City police department."

Carson stumbled into the table, "The police department?"

"Ma'am, I need you to come to Carver Memorial Hospital. Your husband and son have been involved in an accident."

"What? An accident? Are they... are they, ok?" She asked, her words strained and breathless.

"You need to come here, do I need to send someone to get you?"

Carson's gut churned, she knew it must be bad if he was avoiding the question, "No, I'll be there in twenty minutes."

She disconnected the call and grabbed her keys. Slipping her phone into her pocket, she raced out the door and peeled out of her driveway. Her heart nearly beat out of her chest. She knew that bike would get him killed, they fought relentlessly about Max riding with him. And now, as she pulled into the parking lot of the emergency room, the tears streamed down her face as she anticipated the worst. Throwing her car in park, she rushed through the entrance towards the nurse's station.

"Please," her words breathless from running from her car, "My husband and son – they were in an accident."

A uniformed officer approached her, "Mrs. Harding?"

Carson glanced towards the young man's face, his expression filled with sorrow.

"Yes – you called me?"

"I did, let's sit down." He motioned towards the chairs.

"No... please – where is my son?"

"Mrs. Harding, your husband, and son were in a bad accident. I'm afraid," Carson cut him off.

"NO! Please... is he? Is he..." her sob bubbled from her throat, bursting out like a shaken soda.

"Ma'am, your husband has minor injuries. A broken arm, and some cuts. Your son," He took a deep breath, "I'm afraid your son is worse. He was thrown from the bike and is in surgery."

"No... no..." Carson couldn't see, her vision was blurry.

"Mrs. Harding? Are you ok?"

"I..." Her head spun, it was hard for her to breathe.

"MRS. HARDING," she heard the officer call out to her as darkness clouded her mind.

SHIT!" Jason had just come through the doors of the ER when he saw the woman collapse. The officer in front of her reached out, trying to grab her before she fell, but barely grabbed hold of her arm. Jason darted to where she was falling and caught her in his arms.

"Get a nurse!" He snapped at the young officer. He carefully laid her down on the floor, assessing her vitals. She'd only passed out. "What the fuck did you say to her?" He glared at the police officer now standing behind him with several nurses rushing around him towards the unconscious woman.

"I," he rubbed his hand behind his neck, "I asked her to sit – she wouldn't. Her husband and son were in a motorcycle accident. I just told her that her son was in surgery."

Jason looked at the woman, realization hitting him. She was the mother of the boy he'd pulled from the ditch. She started to rouse, her eyes finding his, "What happened?" The nurse helped her up slowly.

"You passed out, ma'am. Take your time getting up." The nurse gripped her hand, tugging her to a standing position. She wavered on her feet.

"My son... oh," her tears spilled down her face, "please... can someone tell me where he is?"

"He's in surgery still. I can take you to your husband."

"No," she jerked her hand from the nurses, "I couldn't care less if he was dead. I just want to see my son."

Jason found it interesting that she'd spoken so aggressively about her husband, there was a story there, but now wasn't the time to ask.

"Ma'am," Jason moved a little closer to her, "My Name is Captain Jason Hunter. I was one of the firemen that responded to the accident scene."

"Can you tell me if my boy was hurt badly?"

"Um," his gut tightened, just as he was going to reply a doctor came through the closed doors separating the waiting room from the back.

"Is there a Mrs. Harding here?"

"Me," she turned from Jason, "I'm Mrs. Harding."

He reached out, shaking her hand, "I'm Dr. Graham. Do you have family with you?"

"No – I don't have any family. My brother is a Marine and deployed overseas. Why?"

"Let's go in back."

She nodded, "Oh," turning towards Jason, "Thank you. Please wait for me, I'd like to talk to you – if you can."

"Sure, I can wait a few minutes. Go – I'll be here when you're ready to talk."

He watched her as she followed the doctor through the double doors. He wanted to reach out and tell her it was going to be ok, but deep down he knew her life was about to change – and not in a good way.

Carson followed the doctor to a small waiting room. She wasn't even sure what floor they were on anymore. She'd been so lost in thought, she hadn't paid attention, only walking in a daze behind him.

"Please, sit." He motioned to an empty chair. Sitting down, he took the seat across from her. "Mrs. Harding,"

"Carson. Please call me Carson."

Smiling he tilted his head in acknowledgment, "Your son and husband were brought into the ER around 4:20pm. Your husband sustained a broken arm and severe lacerations – he is getting a cast as we speak."

"I don't care about my husband-...please, just tell me about Max."

The doctor looked at her, stunned, shaking his head, "Yes – Max. His condition is not good. He was thrown from the bike, both legs were broken at the femur, his right forearm was shattered, and he suffered a massive head injury." Carson sucked in a breath. She fought to keep the bile rising in her throat from spilling out. Dr. Graham continued speaking. "He was taken to surgery right away. Carson, I need to prepare you for the worst. They will be in surgery for hours. The surgeon must alleviate the pressure around his brain first. Once he's stable enough, they'll place a metal rod – one in each leg. His arm was shattered in several places. Hopefully, they will be able to remove the bone fragments and place a rod to stabilize it so it can heal. But," he removed his glasses, "it could all be in vain. Mrs. Harding, Carson, his head injury is severe. You need to understand he may not wake up – and if he does, he may not be the boy you remember." Dr. Graham reached out and grabbed Carson's hand. "Is there any way to get ahold of your brother? It's obvious your husband and you have some issues to deal with, but you're going to need someone to lean on."

"I…" Carson brushed a tear from her cheek, "yes. I can call his CO. My husband and I fought earlier. He… he stormed out of the house. This is my fault. If I'd just ignored everything, he wouldn't have done this."

"You can't blame yourself. He was driving. He made a choice to put your son on the back of the bike – not you. It's going to be hours before they're done in surgery. Go home. They'll call you."

"No – I can't go home with him here. I'll go call my brother." Carson stood. "Where are we?"

"This is the fourth floor. It's where the nurses will bring Max after he is out of surgery."

Carson glanced at the wall, noting the sign that read critical care unit. The words echoed in her mind, reminding her how bad this was. "Doctor," Carson turned to look at him, "Can you tell me where my husband is?"

"He wasn't as bad, so he's still in the ER."

"Does he know about Max?"

"Yes – he didn't take it well."

"Good." Carson left the doctor standing in the corridor as she boarded the elevator. Pressing the floor for the ER, she clenched her fists. She wished it was Phillip laying on the surgery table, not Max. Her son was her whole world – and that world was spinning off its axis.

"Where is my son." She could hear Phillip's voice as she rounded the corner.

"Phillip," Carson stopped at the edge of the desk. She took in his appearance. He had road rash on his arms and his cheek. He had a cast that extended up to his armpit. Stitches adorned his forehead, and he was covered in dirt and blood.

"Carson," he rounded the desk and grabbed her arm. "Where's Max?"

"Let go, you're hurting me." Carson tugged her arm, trying to free herself from his grip.

"I asked you a question. Is Max still in surgery? This bitch won't tell me anything."

"Phillip. Let. Me. Go."

"NO! Not until you tell me where my son is!"

Jason watched as the woman approached Phillip. He was the father of the little boy fighting for his life – and from his spot in the waiting room, it was apparent he was an asshole. Jason watched stunned as Phillip grabbed his wife by the arm. He heard her tell him to let go but watched as he tugged her harder.

Unable to control the protector in himself, he stood and slowly approached the couple.

"Phillip. Let. Me. Go."

"NO! Not until you tell me where my son is!"

"She said let her go," Jason wrapped an arm around Phillip's good side and gently tugged him until he released her arm. "Mrs. Harding, are you alright?"

Carson was rubbing her arm where Phillip's handprint reddened her skin.

"Yes – thank you, Captain."

"Who the fuck are you? This doesn't concern you." Phillip growled behind him.

"Phillip, this is one of the men who worked your accident. He found..." she took a deep breath, "he found Max."

"Oh," Phillip shuffled his feet, "thank you. Carson, please. Nobody will tell me anything about Max."

"I'll go. I just wanted to make sure he wasn't hurting you."

"Wait." Carson touched his arm, "Stay. You saved him. You deserve to hear this as well. If it weren't for you, we might not be having this conversation."

He nodded, pointing towards the chairs in the waiting room, "Let's sit."

Jason took a seat near the window. He watched as Carson seated herself next to him, in a chair that prevented Phillip from sitting next to her.

She drew in a deep breath, "He is in surgery – has been for the last," glancing at her watch, "three hours." She began to fill us in on his condition, fighting the tears that threatened to spill once more. It pained him to see her going through this, it angered him to see her husband provide no form of support.

"Are you fucking kidding me right now?" Carson had her eyes frozen on a woman who'd come through the entrance.

Jason turned, glancing between the two women, "Do you know her?"

"She's the reason my son is fighting death."

He didn't know what to say. Phillip bristled in his chair, obviously uncomfortable with the situation. He knew whoever she was, this was about to get nuclear.

5

The tension was palpable in the waiting room. He stood, "I should go." Slipping his card from his wallet, "Here's my card. If you need anything, please don't hesitate to call me. I hope your son pulls through."

Taking the card from his grasp, Carson snorted a laugh, "What, running away before you can watch my husband's mistress coddle him?"

Jason stood, shocked. His brain processing what she had just said.

His mistress?

She'd called the newcomer her husband's mistress.

"Um. No, it's not that..." he glanced towards her husband, who was now huddled with the woman in the corner.

"Fuck it. I'm going back upstairs to wait for the doctor to come out of surgery.

Thank you for everything you did. Your men, you... I owe you all everything."

She turned, leaving him to watch her retreat. She stormed through the double doors, the sound of them slapping together brought him back to the present. He turned to see Phillip pressing a kiss to the mystery woman.

As he was leaving, Phillip called out to him, "Captain," Jason turned towards him, "I wanted to thank you again. It was an accident, I would never put my son in harm's way."

The anger he had been suppressing bubbled to the front, "If that were true, you would have fitted him with the appropriate helmet. Then maybe he wouldn't be fighting so hard to live."

"You don't know shit."

"I know enough. I know the helmet Max wore was not made for him. I know you betrayed your marriage. I know you'll have to live with the guilt of killing your child for the rest of your life."

"You don't know if he'll die."

"I know he'll never be the same – you might as well have killed him. His life is forever ruined because of what? Her? You're an idiot."

Jason turned and stormed out of the ER. He couldn't believe he'd let his emotions get to him. Slipping his leg over his motorcycle, he wanted to storm back into the hospital and punch Phillip, but he knew that would only make matters worse for Carson. His heart beat against his chest thinking about her. She was beautiful and didn't deserve to go through this alone. He wondered if she'd called for her brother. He had some buddies in the Marines, he knew how hard it was to contact them when they were in country. Shaking his head, he cranked the engine. Tugging his helmet on, he eased out of the parking spot. He needed some distance to gain clarity. He shouldn't feel so connected to a stranger, but something about the way she smiled at him tugged at his heart.

Pulling into his driveway, he dismounted his bike and rolled it into the garage. As he stepped into the foyer, his phone vibrated in his pocket. Glancing at the screen, he pressed talk, "Stoner, what's up?"

"Hey, man. Going out to grab some drinks. Wanted to see if you'd come."

"Yeah... actually, I could use a few. Where we meeting?"

"Crimson Pub."

"Alright, be there in twenty." Glancing at his watch, he realized it was almost nine. He'd been at the hospital for several hours. Turning on his heel, he mounted his bike once more and navigated towards the pub. It was a local hang out for a lot of public safety folks.

Pulling into the crowded lot, he found Stoner's truck. He parked and hurried inside, eager for a drink. He needed to drown away the day in beer.

"Hunter!" Stoner called out from a corner booth. Jonesy was seated across from him, chugging a mug of beer.

"Stoner, Jonesy." Jason slid into the booth next to Stoner. "Pour me one." He motioned towards the pitcher in the middle of the table.

"Bad day?" Jonesy smiled, "Oh, wait. You went to the hospital to see that kid, didn't you?"

"Yeah – it's not good."

"I'm surprised he even made it to the OR."

"He's lucky we found him when we did, or he might not have had the chance."

"What kind of mom lets her husband ride around with a kid in the wrong helmet."

"I don't think she did."

"What do you mean?"

He began filling them in on his hospital experience. He told them how the husband nearly squeezed the life from her arm and then topped it off with his girlfriend showing up.

"Shit – his girlfriend came to the hospital. That's pretty fucked up." Stoner swallowed down his drink.

"Yeah. Is his wife ugly or something?"

"No. Actually, Carson's pretty hot. Phillip's a moron. I don't know what their story is, but she doesn't have any family here. I feel bad for her."

"Oh, no... Hunter, I know that look." Jonesy laughed, "You're going to try and be her hero, aren't you. Man," he slid a glass of amber liquid towards Jason, "you need to steer clear of that train wreck." Just as he was going to reply, the waitress interrupted them.

"You guys want to order something else?"

Stoner smiled up at her, "Sure thing, sweetheart. How about an order of wings and another round of beer...and maybe you could join us?"

"Cute, but my shift isn't over until one."

"I got all night." He smiled bigger. The waitress blushed as she walked away.

"Damn you're such a player." Jonesy laughed.

"You're just jealous since you have a ball and chain and can't play anymore."

"I'm definitely not jealous. In fact," he glanced at his watch, "she just got off work and is waiting on me at home. So," tossing money on the table, "I'll see you in a few days."

They watched as Jonesy left. Stoner was the first to speak, "He's right, you know."

"Right about what?"

"The woman. You should just forget about her. It sounds messy – that's too much work."

"Maybe. I don't know. You're probably right. Alright, I'm going to head out. You coming?"

"Oh, I plan on coming alright – but it'll be after one o'clock." He smirked.

"Good luck with that." Jason smiled as he walked out of the pub. He knew the guys were probably right about Carson. But Jason wasn't sure he could just forget about her or her son. He'd call the hospital in the morning and see if there was any update on the boy. Maybe then he could put them out of his mind.

Carson sat at her son's beside staring at his frail body. He was connected to wires and tubes, a machine sat off to the side of him breathing air into his body. Life support. That's what the doctor had called it – he'd told her that there was a chance he'd never live without it, but they wouldn't know for a while. Max's body was fighting to survive. Carson bent her head, allowing the tears to wet his linens. Her life was destroyed in more ways than she could count.

"Mrs. Harding?" the night nurse roused her from her semi-sleeping state. It was morning, the sunlight streamed through the windows in Max's room. She'd been at his bedside for nearly thirty-six hours.

"Yes?" Carson sat up, stretching her back.

"You should go home and get some rest. I have your number in case something changes."

"No. I can't leave him. What if he wakes up and I'm not here?"

She placed her hand on Carson's arm, "Carson, may I call you that?"

"Yes. Please. We'll be spending a lot of time together." Carson gave her a weak smile.

"Yes – and that's why you need to go home. Get yourself a shower, clean clothes, and then come back. A few hours won't change anything. He will need you at your strongest when he wakes up."

Carson knew she was right, but it felt wrong, leaving him alone. She hesitated, "I know you're right, but I can't leave him. Not yet." As she uttered the words, Phillip walked into the room. Carson glanced at the nurse, "You know what, I think you're right. I'll be back in a couple of hours. Call me if something changes."

"I will." The nurse glanced at Phillip and then back to Carson, "Go get some rest, Carson."

"Carson, wait." Phillip reached out to grab her, but she moved out of his grasp.

"What, Phillip?"

"We should talk."

"What's there to talk about? You nearly killed our son on the back of your stupid bike... then your fucking mistress shows up in the ER. I am pretty sure we have nothing to talk about." Moving into the hallway, she heard him call out to her.

"Please. Carson. Wait a second."

"No – I need to get home and get back in case he wakes up."

"I called an attorney." Carson stopped in her tracks.

"What?" She spun to face him.

"I called an attorney. I'm filing for divorce."

"Good." Carson turned and hurried towards the elevator. She needed to go by the attorney's office she'd scheduled to meet with. But the accident caused her to miss the appointment. Now, she desperately needed to go and talk with her. Phillip had filed for divorce. Max wasn't awake, and that son of a bitch had gone and filed to dissolve their marriage.

She found her car parked in the emergency room parking lot, where she'd left it days ago. She pulled from her parking space and navigated towards downtown. Shower and fresh clothes would have to wait – she needed to hire an attorney fast. She found herself parked in front of Anderson and Quincy, Attorneys of Law. She sucked in a deep breath and went inside. After an hour, she stepped into the sunshine. The attorney had essentially said she was not going to lose a thing – regardless of the fact he'd filed first. His affair ensured Carson would get an excellent settlement. But that didn't matter to her – not if Max died. She found herself seated on a park bench outside her newly hired attorney's office. She knew she should go home, what little was left of it. Glancing around at the tiny town, she wondered what she would do with her life. Phillip had been all she'd known. He didn't want her working, now she knew why. She took care of Max, so he could fuck around.

Glancing off into the distance, she saw she was near station six. She wondered if that was the station that Captain Hunter worked out of. No sooner had she thought about him, he appeared outside the open bay door. He was wearing only a pair of shorts, his chest was bare, she continued to watch as he started off in a jog. She couldn't take her eyes off him. He caught sight of her, slowing to a stop in front of where she sat.

"Carson." He smiled at her, "good to see you again." He looked around, realizing where she was. "Everything ok? With you, I mean?"

"Phillip filed for a divorce," Carson said matter of fact. "Can you believe that son of a bitch filed for a divorce?"

She shook her head, "I'm sorry. I shouldn't be telling you about my problems. I'll be fine. Thanks for asking. How about you? You on duty?"

"Not for a few more hours. I like to come in and get in a workout. Never know if we'll be busy or not."

Glancing at her phone, "I should probably go. I need to shower – God, I probably look and smell awful."

"You look beautiful," Jason smiled, "Look, I know it may be weird, but if you need anything – let me know. I'm here for you."

Carson smiled at him, "Thank you. I put a call in to my brother's commanding officer. They're trying to locate him. When they do, he'll come home for emergency leave. He's all the family I have."

"Well, you have my number if you need anything. Use it if you need anything."

"Ah, thanks." Carson tilted her head, "I should be going." She stood, rubbing her hands across her pants, "Thank you."

"You're welcome." Carson hurried to her car, He watched her pull off the curb and waved. He wanted to spare her from any more pain, but she was hesitant to let him help her. He'd be there when she called, that's all he could do for now.

7

Carson pulled into her driveway. The house looked empty, Phillip's car wasn't in the garage, which meant he was still at the hospital – or with Diane. She scoffed. Diane could have him.

When she walked inside, she immediately sensed something was off. She bolted up the stairs to hers and Phillip's room. Pushing the door open, she knew what was different. Phillip had cleaned out his belongings. Drawers were open and empty. She flung open the closet to find only her clothes. Grabbing a pair of jeans and t-shirt, she slammed the door shut. She wouldn't let him get to her. She needed to get back to Max. Rushing she showered and put on her clean clothes. She glanced at her reflection in the mirror and shuddered. Her hair was wet and hung limply against her shoulders. Black rings adorned her once bright green eyes. Pulling her brown locks into a tight pony-tail she splashed water on her face. No amount of makeup could hide the pain she felt right now. Carson turned off the light and headed back downstairs. She grabbed her keys and locked the door behind her. The ride to the hospital was silent, leaving her alone with her thoughts. A gnawing feeling in her gut had her rushing inside the hospital. When she reached the elevator, she pressed the button with urgency. As she stepped into the metal box, her phone vibrated with a message.

Phillip: Get back to the hospital NOW!

Her: In the elevator.

Carson bounced on her feet, watching the floor numbers count upwards. As soon as it stopped on the fourth floor, she bolted out, rushing towards Max's room. When she pushed through the doors, she found Phillip in a chair, the doctor standing next to Max's bed.

"What? What's happened?" Carson ran to the edge of his bed, pulling his tiny hand in hers.

"Mrs. Harding," the doctor spoke, "please sit down."

Carson nodded, pulling a chair to his bedside. "What is it?"

"We got his scans back." The doctor removed his glasses, "I'm afraid it's not good."

"What does that mean?" Carson looked at Phillip, who sat, tears rolling down his face.

"His scans show no brain activity."

"Is it just too soon? Maybe a few more days will help. Right? It's just too soon." Carson began rocking back and forth. "Please... what are you saying?"

"I'm so sorry, Mrs. Harding. He won't wake up. The machines are keeping him alive."

"NO...NO you're wrong. He's going to wake up."

"He's not." Phillip moaned from his seat, "He's gone, Carson."

"This is your fault, Phillip. You had to have that fucking bike – I asked you not to put him on it... But you didn't listen. You never listen." Carson sobbed.

"MY Fault? This is your fault. You couldn't just leave things alone. YOU DROVE ME TO CHEAT. You're a shitty wife and a terrible lay." Phillip screamed.

Carson stood, looking at the doctor, and back at Max. She couldn't stay in the room, she felt as though she was suffocating. She turned, rushing towards the door, the doctor calling out her name as the door slammed behind her. Carson pressed the elevator button, willing it to open. She flung herself inside, pounding her hands against the metal walls. When the door slid open, she ran, not caring where her feet took her. She was alone – truly alone. She wished her brother were here. He'd shield her from Phillip's hateful words. She found herself outside the emergency room, the sun shining on her face as she screamed to the sky. Her brain couldn't comprehend what was happening. Dropping to her knees, the pavement scraping her flesh, she sobbed. Her tears unabashed for anyone to see. Lost in her sorrow, she didn't hear her name being called. Nor did she feel the arms wrap around her, lifting her off the ground. Her body shook with her grief.

Jason had just emerged from the ER and was stunned to see Carson crumpled on the asphalt. He'd assisted the paramedic in transporting a drowning victim, so his being there at that moment was pure chance. He called out to her as he approached. She was so consumed with grief she didn't hear him. He couldn't stand seeing her so broken. Looking over his shoulder, "Ackers," he called out to the paramedic on shift, "I'll call Chief to come get me, y'all head out, ok?" Ackers looked at him, then to the woman on the ground.

"You need any help?" She quirked an eyebrow at him.

"No – she's a friend. Her son was the boy in the motorcycle accident." He shook his head, jogging towards Carson.

"Alright – I'll tell the guys. Squad will probably come to get you. Don't bother Chief. I'll get you a ride."

"Thanks, Ackers."

He squatted beside Carson, "Carson," he called her name as she sobbed, the tears falling like raindrops, he wrapped his arms around her, lifting her from the ground. He carried her over to a bench nestled against the building. Adjusting her in his lap, he brushed a few fallen strands of hair from her face. Her eyes began to focus, and she looked shocked to see where she was.

"Hunter?"

"Yeah – I got you." He pressed her head against his chest, her sobs came out harder, wetting his shirt. He held onto her for what felt like an eternity before her cries subsided.

"You want to talk about it?" Jason probed her, knowing it had something to do with Max, "Is it Max?"

"Yeah," her voice cracked, "He...he..." she bellowed, burying her head into his shoulder, "He's brain dead."

"Oh god, Carson," he brushed her hair, toying with her ponytail, "I'm so sorry."

"My son's dying or dead. My husband filed for divorce. And he blames me for everything."

"Oh, sweetheart," adjusting her on his lap, looking into her eyes, "it's not your fault. None of it. He made a choice to cheat. He made a choice to put your son on the back of a motorcycle without the proper helmet. None of this is on you."

"Wait," Carson shuffled off his lap onto the space beside him, "What do you mean, 'he made a choice to put your son on the back of a motorcycle without the proper helmet.' I don't understand?"

Jason held his breath. He thought she knew he wasn't wearing a child's helmet. "Shit – I just assumed you knew."

"I knew nothing, Jason. Phillip and I fought all the time about that damn bike... especially about Max riding with him. I hated it. Are you saying this could have been prevented?"

"I mean, it's possible if Max had been wearing the right helmet, he'd have been less likely to have such a severe head injury. But it was an adult helmet. And when he was thrown from the bike, it came off."

"FUCK!" Carson jumped to her feet, "That bastard has the nerve to blame me. I'm going to kill him."

Carson started towards the ER entrance, "Whoa, hang on a minute. Don't do anything stupid. He isn't worth it."

Carson paused, "You're right. I need to call my attorney. SHIT... I left my phone upstairs. I need to go," Carson grabbed him by the hand, tugging him into a hug, "Thank you." She pressed a chaste kiss to his lips and bolted inside. He stood, watching her run away. He was in trouble. She did something to him, something he didn't expect. As he ran his hand over his face, the sound of a loud horn made him jump. He turned to find Stoner hanging out the window of the squad truck, "HUNTER!!" he waved.

"Yeah – thanks for coming."

"Heard you saved a damsel in distress. Come on, we're hungry. We gotta pick up dinner for everyone."

Giving the doors one last glace, "Alright, let's go."

Jason climbed into the passenger seat, "Look, I know you're the Captain and all, but do you know what you're doing?"

He glared at Stoner, "Stay out of it, Stoner."

"I'm just saying...she's married."

"Not for long. And now she's got to bury her son."

"Shit, that's heavy."

"Yeah – it is. So do me a favor and stop busting my balls."

"Wow – she's really gotten under your skin hasn't she. And you ain't even fucked her."

He punched him in the arm, "Don't talk about her like that. She's special."

"Got it." They rode in silence, not speaking any more about Carson. Jason couldn't stop worrying about her. He had another twelve hours to go before he could see her again. Unless he wound up at the ER, then he'd check on her.

9

Carson was pissed. She pushed open the door to Max's room and found Phillip in the same spot she left him.

"How FUCKING dare, you." Carson snapped at him, causing Phillip's head to snap up.

"Excuse me?"

"How dare you blame me. You let him ride on the back of that dumb ass bike, knowing he was wearing a grown-ups helmet. He'd still be alive if he'd been wearing a helmet for him."

"You don't know that. And if you hadn't started the fight that morning, I'd never have stormed out and picked him up."

"No... you don't get to blame me. You deal with the guilt of causing your son's condition."

"Condition? Carson – he's dead."

"No – not yet. I refuse to believe that there is no hope."

"You can't be serious. We need to turn off the machines, let him go in peace."

"GET. OUT." Carson shoved Phillip, who was now standing, "Find your slut and go to her. I don't want you here. He and I don't need you."

Phillip threw his hands in the air, "Fine... this just makes divorcing you easier. No kid, no ties. Have a fucking great life, Carson."

Carson flung herself into the chair at his bedside, pulling his cold hand into hers, "Please Maxie... Mommy needs you to wake up. We're a team. Remember? CarMax... you said it was our special name."

"Mrs. Harding?" the doctor entered the room, "Can we talk?"

"Look, if you're here to tell me my boy is gone... you might as well leave. I refuse to believe there's no chance. It's only been a few days."

"The scans don't lie."

"I don't care. Rerun them."

He sighed, "We can give it a few days. Rerun them and compare. But if there is no change, we need to talk about long-term plans. You understand if the scans still show lack of brain activity, the machines are truly all that is keeping him alive?"

"Yes – but I want you to wait more than a few days. I don't want to do anything until I have talked to my brother. And his CO is trying to locate him for me. Can you give me that? Max is all I have left."

"Yes, but you understand his father can request we end support?"

"What? No. He can't do that."

"He can. So I suggest you get an attorney to ensure he can't make any decisions without your consent."

"Phillip has filed for divorce. I do not plan to contest. If giving him everything allows me control over Max, that's what I will do."

"Call an attorney, Mrs. Harding – I've seen things get really ugly when a child is in the middle."

"Thanks. I'll call her now."

Dr. Graham left Carson alone in the room. She found her phone on the side table, snatching it up, she pressed the number she'd stored for Leeann Quincy, her attorney.

"Anderson and Quincy."

"Yes, I need to speak with Mrs. Quincy. This is Carson Harding, it's urgent?"

"Oh, hello, Mrs. Harding. Hold on, I'll transfer you to her line."

"Thank you."

After a brief hold, Mrs. Quincy picked up. Carson explained everything to her attorney, barely taking a breath as she spoke.

"Alright, Carson. I'm going to file an injunction preventing Phillip from making unilateral decisions regarding Max. I am also going to expedite this case and see if a judge will hear it sooner."

"Thank you. I freaked out when the doctor said Phillip could end life support without my consent. I'm just not ready."

"No need for an explanation. I'll call you as soon as it's been filed."

Carson disconnected the call and went to find the head nurse. After explaining the situation, the nurse directed her to the hospital's legal advisor, who had her sign some papers regarding Max's care. She assured Carson they'd dealt with this scenario before and would have Max's best interest at heart.

Carson decided to go home and pack an overnight bag, she planned to stay here as often as she could. As she was leaving the hospital, her cell phone vibrated in her pocket. Fishing it out, she didn't recognize the number but answered anyway.

"Hello?"

"Carson." Her brother's voice filled the line, "What's happened? My commanding officer found me and said I needed to call home, said it was urgent."

"Oh, Zeke." Her voice cracked, "There's been an accident. Max is in the hospital on life support. It..." she took a breath, "it's bad, Zeke.

"Fuck. Ok," Carson could hear him breath deep, "I'll be on the next flight home."

"Thank you."

"Where's Phillip. Let me talk to him."

"Phillip filed for divorce. He moved out."

"WHAT?"

"He was having an affair. I confronted him and he stormed out. He picked up Max from school on his motorcycle, and..." Zeke cut her off.

"Are you telling me Max is on life support because of Phillip? I'm going to kill that motherfucker. He was never good enough for you, Car."

"I know," she hiccuped into the phone, "but there's nothing I can do about it now. He's trying to take him off support. My attorney is trying to prevent that."

"I'll be there in a day. We'll talk more then. I love you, sis."

"I love you too." Carson disconnected. Relief filled her veins. Her brother would know how to handle Phillip. She threw her phone onto the passenger seat and rested her head on the steering wheel. She needed a drink to numb the pain. Resolving herself, she headed towards Crimson.

Jason's shift ended on a dull note. After a few minor Signal 41's, he'd finally gotten some rest. As he headed out towards his bike, Stoner called after him.

"Hey, let's go get a drink."

"I'm going to go by the hospital first. I'll meet you there."

"Fine – go check on your girl."

"She's not my girl..."

"Keep telling yourself that... she might not be yet, but I've never seen you so vested in a woman before."

Flipping him the bird, he mounted his bike and headed towards Carver Memorial. He'd just pulled into the parking lot when his phone rang. Pulling off his helmet, he pressed the phone to his ear.

"What, I told you I'd be there a bit later," he laughed into the phone.

"You need to get here now... your girl is here – and she's fucked up."

"What? Carson's there?"

"Yep... and Harlen says she's been drinking for a while. She can barely hold herself up on the stool but she won't let him or me help her."

"Shit... Ok, keep an eye on her. I'm headed that way." He slung his helmet back on and tucked his cell in his pocket. He peeled out of the hospital parking lot and sped towards Crimsons. When he arrived, he wasn't ready for what he found. Carson had her elbows propped against the bar top, a straw in her mouth, as she rocked back and forth.

Harlen smiled at him as he approached where she was perched on a stool, "She's been going at it for a while. Said she needed to numb her pain."

"Why didn't you cut her off?"

"I did... that's just pineapple juice." Harlen winked at Jason.

"Carson, honey," he stepped up next to her.

"Oh... hey it's you." She poked his chest, "God your chest is so hard. I wonder if the rest of you is hard like that." She ran her finger down his chest and cupped his cock. "Not yet, but I bet I can make it hard." Her eyes found his, and she smiled.

He grabbed her hand, "Sweetheart, you're very drunk. I think I should get you home." He pulled her from the stool, causing her to crash into his front. Slinging a couple of twenties on the counter, he picked her up.

"I can't drive." She giggled.

"I know. I'll drive." He carried her outside, "Give me your keys."

"They're in my pooooocket." She slurred her words. "I needed to numb the pain. My husband hates me, has for a while. My son is dead – and I refuse to turn off the meshanicle lungs. Lots of alcohol was needed. Don't jusdge me." She slurred her words. Jason set her down and fished her keys out of her pants. He opened her car door and helped her inside. After getting her buckled, he dug through her purse until he found her license. He glanced at the address and tossed it back inside her bag. She was nearly asleep by the time he pulled into her driveway.

"Carson, we're here."

"K." came the muffled reply. He hopped out and went around to her side of the car. Opening the door, Carson nearly fell out onto the ground, but he snatched her into his arms before she could hurt herself.

"You're such a good guy, Hunter."

"Jason."

"Huh?"

"Call me Jason. Hunter is my last name. It's what I go by at the station, but I want you to call me Jason."

Carson snuggled against him, "Mm-mmkay."

He unlocked her door and carried her upstairs, pushing open the door he was surprised to see clothes missing. Realizing pretty quickly, it was Phillip's stuff that was gone. He carried Carson to the bed and laid her down. He stripped her shoes and jeans off, leaving her in her t-shirt and panties.

"You need to sleep this off. Ok? I'll get a ride to my bike. Call me tomorrow, Carson."

She shifted, reaching out to grab his shirt as he stepped away from the bed, "Please don't leave me." Her eyes pleaded with him, begging him to stay. They stared at each other, until Jason finally relented.

"Ok. Let me go get a kitchen chair. I'll sit with you until you fall asleep."

"No... please lay with me. I don't want to be alone."

"Carson," he growled, "that's a bad idea. You're drunk and married."

"I'm getting a divorce from that bastard. And yeah, I'm drunk – but I just want you to lay next to me... Please."

Jason couldn't tell her no. He kicked off his shoes and slid into the bed next to her. Her back was towards him. "Ok, go to sleep, Carson. I'm here if you need me."

11

At some point Carson had rolled over. She woke to find herself pressed against a body. Shifting her weight, a strong arm pulled her tighter. At first, she thought Phillip had come home, but then she realized it was the muscular chest of Hunter... or Jason. She remembered bits and pieces from the day before. She'd talked with Zeke, then gone to Crimson. Fuck, she'd drank a lot sitting at the bar. Flashes of Jason carrying her out of the bar trickled into her mind.

"Morning." His warm voice startled her.

"Um...Morning?" She asked questioningly.

"How are you feeling?" He shifted his body, causing her leg to brush against him. She couldn't help but notice there was a lot of him awake.

"Sorry," he tried to move away from her, but Carson locked her legs around his.

"Don't be." She pressed against him, her body yearning for more.

"Carson," he warned, "I shouldn't have fallen asleep like this. But you kept begging me to stay. I should go now."

Carson wrestled with her conscious, the internal debate about what was right or wrong. "I don't want you to leave."

"I don't want to leave. But if I stay... I might do something we both regret."

Carson pushed herself to straddle him, "Jason, I asked you to stay because you make me feel something other than sadness. I know it's probably wrong, but I want you."

He gripped her thighs, "Carson, I want you too... but I think it's too soon. You have enough to deal with. Adding this would only cause you more stress."

She leaned forward, her face inches from his. Carson studied his face, his eyes were an amber color, almost like the orange at sunset. His skin was a beautiful shade of caramel. Carson couldn't resist her desire anymore. She pressed her lips to his. He froze, unsure of what to do, but instinct took over and he ran his tongue over her bottom lip. Carson moaned into his mouth as he deepened the kiss. "We should stop," he murmured against her mouth.

She responded by reaching down and fisting his erection through his shorts. Jason hissed, squeezing his eyes shut, "Fuck." Carson tugged at his pants, trying to get them off.

"Carson, you should stop – I won't be able to control myself. If you don't want this, you need to stop."

He pushed at her, refusing to let her make a mistake, "I'm sorry, Carson." He stared at the ceiling, "we can't do this. You're married. You don't need me to complicate things." He shifted so his feet were off the bed. As he stood, tightening the string to his shorts, his dick still semi-hard. Grabbing his shirt from the floor, he pulled it over his head. "I should go."

"Jason," Carson watched him, "I want this," she motioned between them, "You...

You're doing something to me. Is the timing, right? No, but I don't care."

"You don't know what you're saying. It's only been a week, Carson. A week since you found out your husband was cheating. A week since the accident. I just think your judgment is a little clouded and I'm sorry, I should go. Look, call me later. I need to go."

"At least let me drive you."

"I already called an Uber." He slipped his phone back into his pocket.

"Fine. Go. I don't care." Carson rolled over and faced the wall.

"Carson – don't do that, please. I'm only trying to watch out for you."

"Just leave, HUNTER." She gritted out his name.

She'd reverted to calling him by his last name, like everyone else. Shit, he'd fucked up. Walking out of the room, he pulled her door shut. He headed down the stairs and opened the front door, only to be greeted by a very large man in dress blues.

"Who the fuck are you?" the stranger demanded.

"I should be asking the same thing." Jason folded his arms across his chest.

"I'm Carson's brother, Zeke."

"Thank god. She needs you right now. I'm Jason Hunter," he thrust his hand out, "I'm a fireman here in Carver. I worked her son's accident. We've become... friends."

"Friends?" Zeke appraised him, "Just friends?"

"Look. Would I like more, I'd be lying to you if I said no. Your sister is a beautiful woman. But she has a lot going on and I just want to be here for her. That husband of hers is a real piece of shit. She had no one... at least she didn't." His Uber pulled into the driveway, "I need to get going. Tell Carson to call me. She's mad right now, but when she calms down, she'll see I'm only trying to protect her."

Zeke watched Jason for a moment, "You love my sister, don't you?"

"What? No... we've only known each other for a week. It's a bit soon to say love. Plus, there's that little problem of her being married."

"That will be rectified soon. And when you know you know – love doesn't really have a timetable, so don't deny your feelings for her. You seem like a good guy – and she deserves one of those." Nodding towards the car in the driveway, "Alright, I'll let you catch your ride. See you around... don't be a stranger, Jason."

He gave a slight nod and hurried towards the waiting car and climbed in. He watched as Zeke stepped inside and shut the door. Jason was glad he was home, Carson needed someone who would help her without clouding her decisions.

Zeke's voice filled the room, "Carson," causing her to topple out of the bed.

"Shit, are you ok?" Zeke pulled her from the floor, wrapping his arms around her. Carson couldn't hold in her tears any longer.

"Thank God. Oh Zeke, I don't know what to do!"

"Shhh... take a breath. I met your boyfriend outside."

"What? I don't have a boyfriend," her cheeks pinked with embarrassment.

"You may not realize it, but you do. Hell, he doesn't even realize it – but I saw how protective of you he is. Friends don't get like that. But we'll cross that bridge when we get to it. Tell me about what happened."

Carson spent the next thirty minutes recounting everything to her big brother.

She was so glad he was here and could help her stand against Phillip. She knew it was only going to get uglier between them.

"Get dressed. I'm going to change my clothes, then we're going to see my nephew."

"We can go later, you have to be exhausted."

"Nope. I slept on the plane. Plus, I'm used to very little sleep. Marine, remember?"

"Yeah, yeah. Ok. I need to shower really fast."

"You sure do. You smell like a liquor distillery, little sister." Carson hurled a pillow at her brother as he darted across the hall. She quickly grabbed a sundress and headed into the bathroom. She couldn't stop thinking about what had happened with Jason this morning. She'd wanted him, and he'd refused. She was mad, but deep down she knew she had no reason to be pissed. He put her feelings first. She'd felt how hard he'd gotten beneath her – yet he managed to resist. That had to speak to the kind of man he was. Something she was not used to. Rushing down the steps, she found her brother Zeke waiting in the kitchen.

"You ready to go?" Carson asked.

"Yes. What are the odds I will have to kick your shitty husband's ass today? I know I said I wasn't tired – but I'm not sure I could handle dealing with that bull-shit just yet."

"I don't know. He stormed out of Max's room and said I could deal with it myself... that we no longer existed to him." Carson's sob bubbled up from her chest. Zeke pulled her into his embrace.

"It's going to be alright, Carson. I will be here for as long as I need to be."

"You don't understand..." she pressed her face against his chest, "The doctor said it's hopeless. Phillip is going to try and force me to turn off the machines. I'm not ready yet – it's only been a week. I need more time... even if it's to say good-bye to my son." Her tears poured from her.

"Let's go see Max. I want to talk to this doctor myself."

They arrived at the hospital in no time. Carson took a deep breath, "All right, let's go."

The nurse who was assigned to Max's main care greeted them at the door to his room. "Carson, I am glad to see you look a bit rested – and you brought someone with you."

"Yes – this is my brother, Zeke. He's in the Marines home on emergency leave."

"Good Morning, ma'am," He shook her hand.

"I'm glad she has someone else to support her through this. Carson, I'll go call the doctor. Let him know you are here."

"Thank you." She placed her hand on the door handle, "You ready? He doesn't look like you remember."

Zeke covered her hand with his, "Let's go."

Carson watched as her brother, a man who'd fought wars and killed people, crumble to pieces. He rushed to the edge of Max's bed and kneeled. He took the fragile boys hand in his and pressed his fingers to his lips.

"Little man, its Uncle Zeke. Your mom and me are here. Can you hear me?" Zeke turned to look at Carson, "What the fuck happened, Carson? I know you said an accident... but," he shook his head.

"He wasn't wearing a child's helmet. Phillip had put him in an adult helmet. The doctor said if he'd been in the right one... maybe," she snorted, half tears, half laugh. "It doesn't matter – what if won't bring him back."

"I'm going to kill that fucker. He best not come here."

"He's not worth it. Diane can have him and all his assholeness." As she spoke the doctor came in and greeted them. Carson and Zeke spent the next hour talking with him about Max's prognosis. Carson listened, knowing in her gut time wasn't going to change anything. Her little boy was gone.

Jason found himself picking up extra shifts. He needed to keep himself busy or else he'd find himself at Carson's house – and he didn't need to be around her. His emotions were all over the place. Her brother Zeke had mentioned love to him, and since he couldn't stop thinking about it, his words hung. Did he love her? Was that even possible – after just a week? He wasn't sure... but the more he toyed with it in his head, the more he couldn't deny there was something about her. His heart stuttered when his team mentioned her name. He'd snapped so many times at them, that they stopped asking. Two weeks had passed since he'd been to her house.

Two. Long. Weeks.

"Hey, Captain." Chaz called out from the bay, "Someone's here to see you."

He tossed the equipment he'd been messing with onto his desk and made his way towards the open bay. He jerked to a stop when he saw Zeke standing alone inside the open space. He was propped against the fire truck, with his arms folded across his chest.

Jason quickened his pace, "Zeke, right?" He thrust his hand into his.

"Yeah – hope you don't mind me stopping by. Carson's across the street signing some paperwork. Her dick of a husband is refusing to give her anything."

"Damn... that sucks. But I'm guessing you didn't come here for that. What's up?"

"Look, I get why you're keeping your distance... I do. But she misses you. And before you go saying you only knew each other a week... you did more for her in that time, than her husband did in seven years."

"Fine... but that doesn't explain why you're here."

"She's going to need you. I can only do so much for her when it comes to the emotional stuff being her brother. But...

with what's about to happen – she'll need someone who can hold her while she cries. And I won't be able to do that."

"What do you mean – with what's about to happen?"

"Phillip convinced a judge he had just as much right to make decisions about Max."

Jason knew what was coming, he clenched his fist at his side, waiting for Zeke to say the words.

"She's turning off life support tomorrow. The judge ordered a battery of tests – which came back the same way they did the first time. My nephew is brain dead. Carson isn't happy about this, hell neither am I, but I know it's time to say goodbye," Zeke chocked back his emotions, "this is going to be hard for her – because she hoped he'd wake up."

"I'm sorry to hear it didn't work out. I'd prayed that the little guy would get a miracle. But I don't understand why you can't be there for her – you're her brother."

"I know... but my time is almost up – and after the funeral, I have orders to return to my duty station. I've held them off as long as I could. But now," Zeke clenched his jaw, "I won't be able to help her, because I won't be here."

"I'm sorry, Zeke. I just don't know."

"Jason... do you care about my sister?"

"Yes. And I know it's far-fetched, but a part of me wants to believe you're right and I love her. But the rational part of my brain reminds me that we'd only known each other for a week."

"And like I said, a week is all someone needs when they meet the person who is meant to be their forever. Don't let society tell you what you feel is wrong. I see it in your eyes when you talk about my sister. She needs someone who looks at her the way you do. Just think about it," Zeke smiled and turned towards the street, "you're a good man. I have a feeling about you and I'm usually never wrong."

Jason watched as Zeke ran back across the street toward the office where Carson was meeting her attorney. It broke his heart to learn she was going to say good-bye to her little boy. She didn't deserve so much pain.

"He's right, you know." Chief Donnelly's voice cut through his thoughts.

"Excuse me, sir?" he turned to face his mentor and friend.

"When you meet the right one, time is irrelevant. When you met this woman, you felt drawn to her – didn't you?"

"Yes, sir – and I know I shouldn't have gone to the hospital that day, but I had to know about the boy. That accident tore me up."

"I know that – hell, I've been in your shoes, son. There have been many accidents I had to know what happened. We don't have that luxury most times. We just handle the scene and send them to the hospital. You did nothing wrong. But don't deny what could be good for you – and for her. I didn't mean to eavesdrop, but I heard her brother. She's going to need someone when he leaves and what little I know about the situation – she isn't going to have anyone."

Chief patted him on the back, "Just think about it, Hunter. It's time you let yourself have something good. I've watched you shut yourself off from life since you lost your parents all those years ago."

"Thanks, Chief." Jason smiled. Donnelly had been there for him when his parents died in a car crash. He'd only been with the department for six months, and Donnelly, who was the truck lieutenant at the time, kept him from going over the edge. Maybe he was right. Maybe he was scared of opening his heart only to have it crushed again. Closing his eyes, he pictured her in his head. Shaking the vision, he knew what he needed to do.

14

Carson sat at the edge of the bed, her eyes closed tightly as she listened to the doctor explain what was going to happen. Phillip had won again. The judge had ordered a battery of tests, then ruled in favor of him. Deep down she knew he had been right, but a part of her hoped for a miracle. A miracle that did not come. Now, as she held onto Max's tiny hand, she let the tears wash down her cheek.

"Carson," Zeke's voice echoed in the room, "Did you hear what the doctor said? Do you have any questions?"

Unable to speak, she simply shook her head yes. If she tried to open her mouth, the scream she was holding in would burst free. Zeke moved to stand beside her, placing his hand on her shoulder.

"Go ahead doc, let's not prolong this any longer." Zeke spoke for Carson, signaling for the doctor to remove the only thing keeping Max in this world.

"Should we wait for Mr. Harding?"

Zeke scoffed, "He won't be coming."

"Very well. I will give you a few minutes before taking him. This is not easy, but you're allowing him to give life to several other children."

He left the room, giving Carson and Zeke time to say their goodbyes. Zeke leaned down and kissed him on the head, "I'll see you again, little guy. We love you." Carson sucked in a breath as he grabbed her hand, "Sis, your turn."

"I..." she looked at her son, leaned in to brush her lips against his forehead, "Little man, I love you. We'll always be CarMax. Mommy will miss you – but I'll see you again. Say hi to grandma and grandpa for me." Her tears fell on his bandaged wrapped head.

"Are you ready?" The doctor had come back in.

"Yes," Zeke nodded.

Carson and he stood, making room for the nurses to unhook his machines and wheel him out. She watched as they ran with his gurney through the hallway, dis-appearing around the corner. She could hear the silent cries of her brother, forc-ing her to look at him.

"Carson," his voice cracked.

"I can't," she jerked out of his grasp, bolting for the elevator doors which had just opened. She had to get out of there.

"CARSON!" She heard Zeke scream as the doors shut. Rushing from the metal box, she fled towards the parking lot. She needed air. Bursting from the hospital, she ran for the grassy area off the side. Collapsing to her knees in the dirt, she let the scream she'd buried in her gut free.

"WHY!" she screamed to the heavens, searching for reason. She buried her face into her hands, the tears and pain shaking her body. Hands wrapped around her waist, lifting her from the dirt to her feet.

"Carson," Jason was there, "CARSON."

She turned to face him, "He's gone... My baby is gone."

He pulled her into his arms, "I know." Brushing his hand down her hair, he rested it on her back.

"There isn't anthing I can say to change that, but you're not alone, Carson."

"Yes... I am. Zeke has to go back in a few days. He's the only family I have."

"CARSON," Zeke came running out of the hospital, "Fuck... what are you doing. I was worried you'd do something dumb." He pulled his sister's arm, turning her to face him. Jason immediately tensed, gripping her tighter.

"Ease up, Zeke. I got her."

Realizing he was hurting her, Zeke released her arm, "Shit. I'm sorry, Carson. I just thought... Look," He looked at her with red eyes, "I can't lose you too. I know this is hard, but you can get through this."

"I just needed air." She whispered, "but I don't know how to do this, Zeke, and you're leaving soon. What then?"

"Then you'll have me." Jason glanced toward Zeke, "your brother made me realize I can't hide away because I worry about how it looks. So, I'll be here for you – if you'll let me."

"I..." Carson stepped from his embrace, "I need some time. Zeke, take me home please. I have a funeral to plan."

Zeke nodded, "She'll need you. Don't let her push you away. Please?"

"Here," he pulled out his card, "my cell number is on this. Let me know if I can help. I'll give her some space – Hell, I walked out and left her two weeks ago. I don't blame her for not trusting me right now."

Zeke took the card and followed his sister to the car. He watched as she climbed into the passenger seat, looking broken. He didn't know how, but he planned to erase that look from her face if he could. He still didn't know if it was love, but he was going to spend the next few weeks finding out.

As Carson and Zeke pulled into the driveway, she immediately spotted Diane's car. "You have to be fucking kidding me."

"What – who's car is that?"

"That, my dear brother, is Diane's car. Which means, Phillip is here." She got out of the car and slammed the door.

"Whoa," Zeke jogged to catch up, grabbing her arm, "slow down. Let me deal with this tool, ok?"

Together they climbed the steps and found Phillip standing in the kitchen.

"What the hell are you doing here, Phillip?" Zeke stood in front of his sister.

"Last time I checked, this was my house." He smarted off.

"You haven't been here in three weeks. Why now?" Carson pushed passed both men and opened the fridge. She retrieved a bottle of wine and set it on the counter.

"I came to drop these off," he tossed a stack papers on the table, "they're divorce papers."

Scoffing, "Are you fucking serious, Phillip? Do you know what I did today? I said goodbye to our son. Your son. You know, the one you killed?"

Phillip moved quickly, grabbing Carson by the throat, "You did that, not me."

Zeke was on him in a flash, jerking him backwards, "Get your fucking hands off my sister."

Phillip pushed him backwards, throwing his hands up, "Don't worry – I'm leaving. Sign the papers, Carson. The sooner we're done, the quicker I can erase this part of my life."

Carson spit in his face, "Fuck you."

He wiped his cheek with the back of his hand, "Cute."

Turning, he left the house, peeling out of the driveway.

"We need to change the locks. Will you be ok while I go to the hardware store?"

"It can wait, Zeke."

"No. It. Can't."

"Fine... yeah, I don't think he'll be back tonight."

"I'll be back in a few," he leaned across and kissed her head, "stay strong, lil' sis."

Nodding, she poured her glass of wine and sat at the table. She heard the car door slam, signaling his departure. She pulled the stack of papers towards her and began reading. Phillip was trying to get out of paying anything, under the grounds they no longer had a child together. She shoved the paperwork away from her, lowering her forehead to the wood table. Carson's mind flashed back to Jason. He'd been there once again when she'd needed someone. But he'd also run away a few weeks ago – avoiding her completely. She couldn't deny how her heart beat a little faster when he was near. And of course, she still wanted him – but her grief over losing her son masked that desire. Looking at the scattered papers, she caught sight of a card. Sliding it towards her she realized it was Jason's departmental card. The one he'd given her weeks ago – with his cell phone number written on the back. She thumbed the card, before slipping it into her purse. When she was ready, she'd call him. For now, she needed to call her attorney.

Thirty minutes later she'd learned her attorney wasn't made aware of the papers. Her guess was Phillip was trying to intimidate her. Glancing at the fridge, Carson decided she needed something to take her mind off the day and stood. She was going to bake something. She'd been meaning to take something to the fire station – maybe she would do that now.

Zeke walked in to find Carson covered in flour. She was rushing around the kitchen like a maniac.

"Um, Carson?" He set the bag he had in hand down on the kitchen table, glancing at the divorce paperwork scattered across the top.

"I wanted to bake." She was beating something in a bowl, the batter splattering everywhere.

"Whoa," Zeke grabbed the spoon, "Sis – you've gotten more batter in the kitchen, than there is left in the bowl. Shit... you're beating that bowl like it's harmed you or something." He took it from her hands and set it down. "Look at me." He grabbed her chin.

"What am I supposed to do? He is taking everything, Zeke."

"We won't let him." He guided her to a chair and began picking up the strewn papers.

"Did you talk to the attorney?"

"Yes, she didn't know about the paperwork. She thinks he did this to intimidate me."

"Fucking prick." Zeke spewed.

Carson chuckled, "yeah... he is isn't he."

Zeke eyed the half empty bottle of wine, "Don't hog that, give me some." She slid the bottle to him and watched as he tipped it to his lips. "Gross. How do you like this shit?"

"I should clean my mess." Carson glanced around the room.

"Nah – leave it. By the way, I talked to the funeral home. Everything is set. Viewing is tomorrow, funeral will be the day after." Zeke swigged the bottle again, wincing as it went down.

"Thank you." Carson tried to smile, "I think I'll go and take a bath." She stood, glancing at the mess she'd made. "I can't do this right now."

"Fine. I'll change the locks and come check on you."

He watched as she left him alone in the kitchen.

Grabbing his phone, he dialed the only person he knew could help her.

"Hey, it's me. Look, I know you said you wanted to give her space – but she needs you. Please." Zeke nodded and disconnected the call. He knew his sister would be mad at him, but he needed someone who could break through the wall she was erecting around herself. He set off to change the locks. At minimum he'd keep her safe from Phillip.

16

Carson stripped down and sunk into the warm bubbles. She wanted to wash away everything – if that was possible. She listened as Zeke ran the power tools. He was installing new locks and adding more deadbolts. She leaned back and closed her eyes, trying to squeeze the memory of her son being taken away from her. She hadn't meant to snap at Zeke – he'd only aimed to help with arrangements. Max's dad was useless after all. Wanting to forget, she sank beneath the surface holding her breath. She imagined Max's face – wishing she could hold him one last time.

"WHAT THE FUCK, CARSON!" She was ripped from the tub by a pair of strong arms.

"What are you doing? Jesus..." A towel was wrapped around her body. She blinked her eyes open, finally focusing them on the man holding her against his body.

"Hunter?" she blinked, "Wha... what are you doing here? In my bathroom?"

"Zeke called me."

"That doesn't explain why you're in my bathroom – holding me naked, might I add."

"I called your name a bunch. When you didn't answer, I thought you might have passed out – you did drink wine. So, I opened the door to check. What were you doing, Carson? You were under water... I thought – fuck, I don't know what I thought."

"Hunter..."

He cut her off, "Jason – please call me Jason again."

"Fine, Jason. I was trying to forget my day. I wasn't trying to kill myself – only wash away the pain. Do you think you could put me down? I'd like to put on some clothes."

He set her on her feet and followed her into the bedroom. Jason bumped into her, noticing her eyes locked onto a picture across the room. It was a picture of Max and her sitting on a blanket in a field.

"He loved picnics." She whispered.

"He was a beautiful little man."

"I miss him." He tightened his arms around her.

Carson leaned into his embrace, "It will get easier. I'll be here to help you."

"Why? You should find someone with less baggage."

Jason spun her to face him, "I don't care about the baggage, Carson."

"You should. I don't know if I can give you what you want or need. I'm broken."

"Lucky for you I like to fix things... but here's the thing, Carson – you don't need fixing. You only need to heal. Let me help you."

"HEY GUYS," Zeke hollered up the stairs, "I'm running out to get dinner – be back in a bit." The front door slammed, bringing them back to the present.

Carson locked eyes with Jason, she knew it was confusing, the feelings she had for him were wrong. But she couldn't deny she felt for this man.

"Carson," her lips pressing against his cut him off. He froze at first but gave into her demands. He walked her backwards, until her knees hit the edge of the bed. Her towel fell to the floor, leaving her naked before him.

"God, you're beautiful."

"Please help me forget – even if it's only for tonight."

Jason pressed his lips to her again and lowered her to the bed. His body covered hers beneath his, "Carson – I know it's too soon. But you need to know this isn't a one-time thing for me... you're too important to me."

Carson gripped the back of his head and pulled him in for a searing kiss. Her hips bucked against him as she pressed her core into the hard outline of his erection.

"You have on too many clothes." She fisted his shirt, trying to tug it off him. He responded by pushing off her and pulling it off in one quick motion. Carson took in his perfectly chiseled stomach. The smooth russet color of his skin begging to be licked. Leaning forward she ran her tongue across his chest. Jason grabbed her hair, tugging her face to his. Carson tugged at his pants, unfastening his belt and snap. In seconds she had his cock freed and in her hand. She moaned as she tried to wrap her hand around his shaft. He grunted, pressing himself into her hold.

"Fuck, darlin'... you're driving me crazy."

Kicking his pants free, he stripped his boxers off and pressed between her legs. "Are you sure this is what you want?"

Carson responded by wrapping her legs around his waist and tugging him closer. She could feel the head of his cock begging to be buried between her heat.

"Sweetheart," He pulled back some, "I need to hear you say it..."

"Yes... please."

"Yes, what?"

"Fuck me, Jason. I need to feel something other than this pain. Please help me to forget."

Jason pressed inside her, easing his firm member between her soft, wet folds. She moaned, closing her eyes in ecstasy. Once he'd buried himself completely, he froze, relishing in the feel of her tight walls wrapped around his dick.

"Please..." Carson moaned, pressing her lips to his shoulder, snapping him from the moment. He pulled back and pressed in, repeating the motion again and again. Carson met his thrusts by bucking her hips against him. He could tell she was close, her body was singing to him as he pounded into her pussy.

"I'm going to come..." She shuttered, her core sucking his cock tight. He paused, letting the sensation of her walls spasming around her. He wanted to stay inside her forever, never stop giving her pleasure. Carson moaned and writhed beneath him. She rocked faster and faster. "Shit... Jason – I'm close again."

He picked up his thrusts, "I'm close, baby." He pressed his lips to hers as she locked her legs around him, burying him deeper inside her. With one last thrust her cunt erupted around him, forcing him to explode with her. "JASON!" she screamed out as his seed filled her to the brim. He paused, feeling the last of her orgasm subside.

"Jesus Christ." He pressed a kiss to her head and rolled onto the bed. He pulled her against him.

"Wow. I had no idea it could be like that."

"What do you mean?"

"Sex – that was... wow. Just wow."

"Come on – you're just saying that."

Carson propped on her elbow, "No – with Phillip, it was about his pleasure not mine. I never had an orgasm by him."

"I really hate that fucker."

Carson snuggled into his shoulder, "Thank you – you helped me forget the pain I felt earlier."

"I'd do anything for you, Carson. Anything."

They laid like that for a few minutes, dozing off until they heard the door open downstairs.

"Come on, let's get dressed. Zeke probably has food and you need to eat."

17

Zeke smiled as Carson and Jason stepped into the kitchen, "So... I guess you two worked through things?"

"Yeah – you could say that." Carson laughed.

"It's good to hear your laugh." Zeke smiled.

Carson stopped, tears welling her eyes, "Shit – that wasn't supposed to make you cry."

"I know – but it's wrong to feel happy when my son is dead. Oh God," she collapsed into a chair. Jason at her side in an instant.

"Stop. You can feel happiness and be sad at the same time. You have every right to mourn Max, but he wouldn't want you to wallow in sadness. He loved you – I love you." Jason watched, holding his breath, as he waited for her reaction.

"You love me?"

"Yes – as crazy as that sounds, I do. A wise man told me to stop hiding from my feelings just because we've only known each other a short time."

"You love me." It was a statement, this time. Carson looked to Zeke, who only smiled and shrugged.

"Maybe I should have held off on telling you, but you need to know you're not alone in this. Ok? I'll be here when Zeke can't be."

Carson leaned into him, pressing her lips to his, "I think I love you too. It's just so soon."

"I don't need you to tell me back. Just let me help you, ok?"

Carson nodded and took a bite of the Chinese in front of her. Closing her eyes, she tried to purge the vision of tomorrow's events from her mind.

"I go on shift tomorrow night at six, but I'll be at the viewing with you and Zeke. And I'll be with you at the funeral. Ok?"

She nodded, unable to say words. Tomorrow she would bid farewell to her precious Max. His life was taken too soon. It wasn't fair.

"I need to go to the attorney's office in the morning. She needs me to sign some paperwork."

"I can meet you there, if you want."

"That would be nice. Zeke will drive me. But I'd appreciate the support. Then we can ride over to the funeral home together." Carson dropped her fork, "I'm sorry." She stood, "I need to be alone." She stood and moved towards the stairs.

"Wait," Jason called her name as he stood from the table.

"No – please. I need some time to wrap my head around everything. I promise I'll be ok."

Jason grabbed her into a hug, "fine, but call me if you need me. You are not alone, Carson. Remember that, ok?"

She pulled away and headed upstairs. She needed some time alone. Grabbing the photo of Max from her nightstand, she sat with it clutched to her chest. She didn't know how she was supposed to carry on. She wanted him here with her. Even if it was for a moment. A moment to say goodbye – even if it tore her heart in two. She laid down, still clutching it against her chest, she cried herself to sleep. Her dreams were filled with memories of Max. Memories she prayed she wouldn't forget when she woke.

"Ummhumm," he mumbled, swallowing his food. "She's stronger than she realizes. When she got pregnant in college, she managed to graduate with a 4.0 anyway. Even with Phillip demanding she stop. He never wanted her to do anything outside of the house. She wanted to believe he meant well, but I knew then he was a prick. When our parents died, he was an even bigger asshole."

"Did her parents die after Max was born?"

"Yes and no – that little guy was a year old when my mom passed. She had cancer. Our dad died about a year later. Heart attack – honestly, I think it was a broken heart. He and my mom had been married

forty years. High school sweethearts."
Zeke tipped a beer to his lips.

"That sucks – at least you had each other."

"Not really – she had to deal with their deaths for the most part without me. I came home for the funerals, then deployed right back out. So, when I say she is strong, I mean it. How about you? Your parents around?"

"No – they died right before I joined the fire academy. Car accident."

"Damn... no siblings?"

"Nope – Chief Donnelly is the only reason I survived their deaths. I was in a bad place and nearly killed myself with alcohol."

"See... I knew there was a reason you two crossed paths. You can heal her, just as much as she can heal you. You know what?" Zeke quirked an eyebrow at Jason, "I think you should stay the night. Screw giving her space. She doesn't know it yet, but she is going to need you. She might be strong... but this is going to be the hardest thing she's had to overcome. Don't get me wrong. I'm sad as fuck. But he wasn't my kid – just my nephew. My hurt isn't like hers."

"Yeah... I hear you. You think me staying is smart?"

"I do. You can be here for her when she needs you."

"Alright, but I need to run home and grab some clothes. I'll come back."

Jason finished his food and headed out. When he got home, he filled his pack with his uniform and grabbed some toiletries. The rest of his gear was stored at the station. It didn't take him long to get back to Carson's. When he pulled in, Phillip stood on the porch yelling at Zeke.

"I said get the fuck out of here."

"This is my house and I have every right to be here."

"No, you don't. Your attorney made it clear you no longer have the right to come and go – you and my sister are officially separated. GO get back in your car, Phillip. Diane is waiting."

Jason jogged up the steps and stood beside Zeke, "Everything ok?"

"Yeah – I was just telling this tool he needed to get gone."

"Oh wow. The fireman is sleeping with my wife now?"

"She's not your wife. And you have a lot of nerve making comments when your slutty homewrecker sits inside the car watching."

"Whatever... you can have her – she's a shitty wife and lay."

Jason saw red, and before he realized what was happening, he had thrust his fist into Phillip's nose. The crunching sound of bones breaking filled the air.

"FUCK! You broke my nose!" Phillip stumbled back. "I'll have your job for this..." He screamed as he ran towards his car. Diane was there waiting for him, handing him a towel to press against the gush of blood running down his face.

"FUCK you prick. Go ahead and try. When you call to report me, be sure to tell them what you said that caused me to break your nose." Jason screamed after him.

"Fuck him, Jason. If you hadn't punched him, I would have. You just beat me to it." Zeke ushered him inside.

"Carson know he was here?"

"No. She's asleep and I wasn't going to wake her for that shithead." Zeke slammed the door and locked it behind them. "We can tell her tomorrow. I'm sure dickweed will be at his own kid's funeral. Though, I'd be ok if he wasn't."

"Me too."

"I'm heading to bed. Tomorrow is going to be a long day."

Jason nodded, climbing the stairs to Carson's bedroom. He waved at Zeke as he shut his door. Jason pushed open Carson's bedroom door unsure of what he'd find. Sucking in a breath, he stepped inside.

18

Jason couldn't believe his eyes. Carson was fully clothed, clutching a photo of Max clasped tightly in her hands, as she laid sound asleep. His heart broke for her. He'd seen so many people bury a child in his career, but this one hurt his heart more. He knew why. It was because he had fallen in love with her.

He kicked off his shoes and stripped down to his boxers. He tugged the covers down, easing her beneath them and then climbed in beside her. He pulled her body to his and held her close. She sighed, snuggling in deeper to his hold. He wanted to shield her from the pain she'd feel tomorrow, but he knew that wasn't possible. Instead, he'd just be there for her.

Carson woke up with something warm pressed against her. She realized it was a body. Rolling over, "Jason?"

He stirred, pressing into her more. "You ok?"

"Um... yes, but can you tell me what you're doing in my bed?"

"I decided to stay. In case you needed me." He pressed a kiss to her head. Carson's eyes welled up. She couldn't believe he'd come back for her. "We should get up. Your attorney will be expecting us in a bit."

Carson rolled from his grasp, realizing she was still dressed, "Shit – I fell asleep like this?"

"Yep." Jason stood and started towards the bathroom. Carson sucked in a breath as she realized he was only wearing boxers. She bit her lip and pressed her eyes shut.

"You go first. I need to find something to wear today." She rushed from the bed and closed herself in the closet. She glanced around, remembering she was burying her son today. Grabbing a pair of black slacks and a gray silk blouse, she crushed them to her chest and slid down to the floor. She couldn't do this.

The closet door burst open and Jason snatched her off the floor, "I got you. You're not alone." He carried her into the bathroom, where he set her down on the toilet. He went back into the bedroom where he retrieved a clean bra and panties. One day he'd strip them off her, but today he'd help her get in them. Taking the pants and shirt from her grasp, he hung them on the back of the door and turned on the shower. "Stand up."

Carson complied, standing so he could strip off her shirt. He tugged her pants down, taking her panties with them. He unsnapped her bra, sliding it down her arms, freeing her breasts. He smiled at her and pushed his boxers to the floor. Lifting her from the floor, he carried her into the shower. The spray hit her on the back as he backed her into the warm water. Using one hand to hold her, he grabbed the shampoo with his free hand. Squeezing a generous amount directly onto her head, he put the bottle back. Gently he scrubbed her scalp and then rinsed her head under the falling water. Carson tilted her head back as he ran his fingers through her locks. Spinning them so he was under the water, he did the same and washed his own head. He then lathered her up with soap, shifting her so he could wash every inch. Carson never let go, her legs firmly wrapped around him. She rested her head on his shoulder as he ran his hand down her back. She was so lost in the moment, she didn't hear the water turn off, only snapping out of her trance when he wrapped the towel around her.

He propped her on the counter, drying her legs and body. Grabbing the panties, he'd brought in, he slid them up her legs, easing her off the counter to pull them up. Her feet pressed to the floor as he steadied her. He handed her the bra he'd chosen and helped her into it. Slipping the blouse over her head, he bent to the floor and eased her feet into the pants.

Once she was completely dressed, he pressed a kiss to her and walked her to the bed. She watched from her perched spot on the edge as he dressed himself. Her

damp hair fell against her ba⸱
ing her she needed to do som⸱
her locks. Snapping from the s
she was in, she started to stand

"Hang on. What are you doing
grabbed her arm.

"I need to do something with m⸱

"Sit," he guided her back to the be⸱
"I'll help you."

He grabbed a brush and a ponytail
holder. Sitting on the bed next to her, he
drew her hair into the fastener. She
couldn't believe he was taking care of her.
"Now, let me help you so you can brush
your teeth and we can go."

They stood side by side, getting ready.
Carson couldn't help watching him in the
mirror. His forearm muscle bunched and
tightened as he brushed his teeth. "You
ready?"

Carson nodded, slipping on a pair of
black flats as they headed down the stairs.
Zeke was waiting on them in the kitchen.
"You guys ready? We can grab coffee after
we meet with your attorney."

They walked out of the house, Zeke
pulling the door shut and securing the

ĸs. Carson froze, her eyes glued to Jan's motorcycle in the driveway.

"You ride a motorcycle?" He could hear the pain in her question.

"Yes."

"Zeke, let's go." Carson ran from him, locking herself inside the car.

"Fuck." Jason shook his head.

"Yeah – I should have told you to hide it in the back. I wasn't thinking."

"It's not your fault. I should have known she would have a bad reaction. I've never had a need for anything else. Until now. Hey look," Jason turned towards Zeke, "I'll meet y'all for coffee when you're done. I need to go take care of something." He hurried down the stairs and got onto his bike. He tore out of the driveway, heading into town. He knew what he needed to do. And he'd do anything for Carson – so this took priority.

Zeke frowned, "You want to talk about it?"

"No." She looked out the widow as Zeke headed into town.

"Come on, Carson. You completely freaked out and left him standing in the driveway."

"He rides a fucking motorcycle. I won't be with anyone who could do something so reckless."

"He's not Phillip, Car."

"I can't lose someone else I love to a two-wheel deathtrap. I won't do it."

"You love him?"

"That's what you heard from that?"

"That's all that matters. Nothing else, Carson. Talk to him. Up until you, he's had no family."

She looked over at her brother, "I can't. Not right now."

They pulled into a parking space close to her attorney's office. Immediately they spotted Phillip and Diane standing near the entrance.

"Great." Carson mumbled as she climbed out of the car.

"Hey – wait for me. I don't want him trying anything. He came by last night, I refused to wake you up."

She looked at him closer, "What the hell happened to his face?"

"Jason happened."

"WHAT?"

"Carson, he said some really bad things about you. If Jason hadn't hit him... I would have."

She and Zeke approached the door, "Phillip." She snarled, "Why are you here?"

"I'm hoping we can come to an agreement. My attorney is inside as well."

"Today... you chose today?"

"It's as good a day as any."

"No. It's. Not. I'm burying your son today. Or do you not care?"

Phillip followed her and Zeke inside. The attorneys were waiting for them as they took their seats at the table. Almost an hour later, they'd managed to work out almost everything. The only thing standing in the way was the house. Phillip wanted her to agree to sell the house and split the profits. She wasn't ready to let it go. Living there was the only reminder of her son. Carson told him she needed more time to decide – inevitably leaving the divorce on hold. She'd gotten his retirement, and a year of alimony, but she wasn't ready to walk away and let him take the house. Getting up from the table, she headed outside. The sun was bright as she stepped out from the dim offices.

"Tell your boyfriend to stay away from me, or I'll press charges next time." Phillip walked up behind her.

"Why do you hate me so much, Phillip?"

"We should have never married each other. I don't hate you... I just never loved you. That boy was all that held me here – and now he's gone. So am I. Sell the house, Carson – you don't deserve to keep it."

"Fuck you, Phillip. I don't want to spend another minute under your shadow or with the reminder of what I lost — but I need time to mourn. The house is all I have left of our son. The son you killed." She regretted the words as soon as they left her mouth.

Phillip grabbed her arm, "Screw you, Carson."

She shook her head, tears spilling down her cheeks, "Let me go."

"No — you bitch. Don't you dare blame me for Max's death. If you hadn't pushed and left things alone, he'd be here today."

He was a piece of work. How had she not seen it before this. "I said, Let. Me. Go."

"I suggest you get your hands off my sister." Zeke stepped up behind Carson, "Or you'll be getting a taste of my fist this time."

Phillip let go of her arm, "She isn't worth it. Get out of the house, Carson. Sign the damn papers so we can be done with each other."

Carson spun, "FUCK you, Phillip. You might hate me, but what about Max?

Don't you feel any pain or sorrow – he's dead! DEAD!"

Arms wrapped around her waist. Glancing up, "Jason," she turned to bury her face in his chest.

"You need to leave." Jason's anger was unmistakable in his voice, "Because the only thing stopping me from laying you out right here, is the fact I'm taking Carson to say goodbye to her son."

Phillip scoffed, "You can have her." He stormed off towards his car without a second glance.

"Nice wheels, brother. Yours?" Zeke eyed the truck behind Jason.

"Yeah. Sorry I wasn't here with you, but when I saw your reaction to my motorcycle, I knew what I needed to do."

Carson inhaled sharply, "You bought this – for me?"

"Yes. Got rid of two wheels for four."

"I don't know what to say." Carson shook her head.

Jason grabbed her hand, "I told you. I'd do anything for you."

"Thank you."

"Can I drive you to the funeral home?"

"Zeke?"

"Carson, you don't have to ask me. I'll meet you guys there." Turing on his heel, Zeke headed towards the car, leaving them to follow him.

Jason helped Carson into the truck, "You ready?"

"No... I don't think I'll ever be ready for this."

The funeral home was filled with so many people, but Jason never left her side. She held it together, longer than she thought she would be able to, before the damn holding her emotions in crumbled.

"I got you." Jason eased her into the truck cab. "I'm going to take you home. Zeke will be there with you. Chief has already approved me coming to the funeral tomorrow. I'll be there for you. Do you hear me, Carson?"

"Yeah." She mumbled, her head resting against the glass. "I can't believe you bought a truck."

"Why does it surprise you that someone would want to do something for you, Carson? Damn, Phillip must have been a real piece of shit. Listen to me," he gripped her hand, "When I love someone, they are the most important thing to me. There isn't anything I wouldn't do for you."

Carson smiled, "I'm learning to accept that part of you. It's new to me. Phillip was a controlling man who only cared about his needs. It's nice to have someone think about mine. I think it's what made me fall in love with you."

"What did you say?" Jason couldn't believe what she'd said.

"I said... I love you, Jason. I know it was fast and probably the worst timing ever. But you've held what little bit of my heart is left, together – when I thought it would crumble completely."

Jason pulled into the driveway and threw the truck in park. He pulled her across the seat into his lap and brushed the strands of hair that had fallen loose from her face. "I love you, Carson." He pressed his lips to hers.

"Phillip wants me to sell the house." She stared off towards the empty house as she spoke.

"WHAT? Why would he want you to do that?"

"He wants the money from the sale. It's why he was yelling at me on the sidewalk."

"What do you want to do?"

"I don't know. It's all I have left of Max... but I think I'm just scared. Where will I go? He never let me work – I have nothing and Zeke will be leaving soon."

"You'll stay with me."

"What?" She turned to face him, "No... Jason." She looked down, fidgeting with her hands.

"Are you serious? Carson," he pulled her chin towards him, "I love you. Move in with me."

She watched him, his eyes pleading with her, begging her to say yes. "I don't know... this is all so fast..." she slid from his lap, "I can't..." she pushed the door open and fled, leaving him to stare at her as she retreated inside.

Slowly, Jason got out of the car and followed her into the kitchen. "Carson," he grabbed her wrist, "Look at me."

"I don't know what to do." She cried, pressing her hands to her swollen eyes, "He's taken everything!"

"Carson... I can't take away the pain of losing Max, but he hasn't taken everything. I'm here. Standing in front of you – telling you I love you."

Carson dropped her hands and stared at the man before her. He had come into her life at the worst possible moment, yet – he was everything she needed. Jason was her lifeline... the only thing keeping her from giving up. She needed him to help her forget, even if it was only for a little while, that her precious son was dead.

Jason smiled, "What do you need, Carson?"

Zeke walked inside, interrupting her response. He was talking to someone on the phone. Carson could tell he was pissed at whoever was talking to him. He tossed his phone onto the table and grunted.

"That bad?" Carson spoke, causing him to jump.

"Fuck, I didn't see you there. Yeah. That was my CO. I deploy Saturday. He said a month was all he could get me." He rubbed his hand down the back of his neck, "I'm sorry, Carson."

Carson forced a smile, but the tears dripping down her reddened cheeks told another story. "I understand."

Zeke rushed to his sister's side, "Liar." He gripped her head, pulling it to his shoulder, "I don't want to leave you – this isn't like mom or dad. I miss him too – I'm not ready to go back either."

"You have to, Zeke. We knew you weren't here forever... plus," she pulled from his embrace, "Jason is here."

Zeke turned to appraise the man standing behind his sister, "Yes. He is." Zeke smiled. "Now, I need to go and pack my stuff up. I have to report to base right after the funeral."

"Zeke," Carson reached out, pulling him in for another hug, "Thank you."

"Anytime. It's you and me, sis. I love you." He pressed a kiss to her head and released her. Turning he ran up the stairs.

"I feel like I'm losing everyone all at one time. My marriage is over. My son is dead. And now Zeke is leaving."

Jason wrapped her in his arms, "I'm here for you. I am not going anywhere unless you tell me to."

She took his hand, "Are you sure you want this mess?" she waved her hands in the air.

"Yes."

She smiled at him, glancing over her shoulder, "Can you help me forget – just for a little while? I need to feel something other than this pain."

"Eat first."

Jason threw a meal together quickly. They ate in silence, the whole time he held her hand in his. He could feel the internal battle she was fighting. Glancing at the clock, he realized he needed to get to the station.

"I don't want to leave you, but I have to go to the station. I'm on shift in an hour."

Carson nodded, realizing it was nearly five, "Shit, I didn't realize how late it was."

Jason stood, pulling her to stand, "Let me take you upstairs and get you settled."

"I don't want to make you late. You've done so much already."

"I have time." He scooped her into his arms and carried her upstairs. He kicked the door shut before tossing her on the bed. He pulled his shirt over his head as he kicked off his boots.

"What are you doing?" Carson eyed his bare torso.

"Helping you forget." Jason covered her body with his as he pressed her into the bed. He nipped her ear, running his lips across her neck.

"Mmmmm," Carson moaned as he sucked just below her chin, her hips bucking against him. Tugging her dress, he slipped it over her head. His hands found the clasp to her bra and released it, freeing her breasts. Tossing it to the side, his mouth found her pink nipple. She let out another moan as he sucked and nibbled it. His lips made their way up, pressing into hers as his tongue found refuge inside her mouth. Carson ran her hands along his shoulders, gripping him as their kisses grew hungrier.

"Pants... off..." she whispered into his mouth.

Jason pushed off her, kneeling on the bed between her legs. He ran a finger across the satin panties, brushing against her clit hidden beneath. Unsnapping his pants, he pushed them down his hips, his cock springing free. Carson reached up and grabbed his shaft, her fingers wrapping around his hardened length. Jason leaned his head back and hissed, "Fuck."

Covering her body with his once more, he pressed his lips to hers. He pressed his fingers beneath the smooth fabric of her undies and buried his fingers inside her soft folds. He worked her pussy, her juices coating his digits as he drew an orgasm free.

"Please... I need you inside." Carson begged, thrusting her hips into his hand. Jason pulled his soaked fingers from her, pressing them into his mouth and sucked her nectar from them. She wiggled, pushing her panties down and kicking them free. Fisting his pants, she pushed the material down, urging him to bury himself inside her. Jason didn't need any further coaxing. With one thrust, he pushed his cock inside her warm center. Carson cried out, the sensation of him filling her was unlike anything she'd remembered. He began thrusting, drawing his shaft in and out. She jerked her hips, wrapping her legs around his waist.

Kissing her, Jason could feel her cunt tensing up. Her walls were gripping his dick like a vice as her orgasm built. "Shit – I'm close, baby. Come with me," he whispered against her lips.

Carson buckled, her pussy spasming as she screamed out. Jason grunted, his dick releasing his seed inside her as he fell over the edge with her. His cock spurted as her walls continued to milk him dry. "Fuck," he pressed a kiss to her forehead.

"I love you, Carson." He slipped his cock from her folds.

"I love you too." Carson draped her arm over her forehead, her eyes closed. Jason pushed off the bed, pulling up his pants.

"Get some sleep, baby." He ran his hand over her leg, leaning down he kissed her ankle. "If you need me call my cell – or the station." Looking at the clock on her bed stand, "I need to go." He scrunched his face, "will you be ok?"

"Yeah – I'm so tired. Plus, Zeke is here."

Jason dressed quickly, pausing at her bedside, he kissed her, "I love you – if you need me, call me. I'm serious."

Carson was already giving herself over to sleep, "mmmhum, I will," she mumbled. Jason tossed the covers over her, pausing to steal one last glance at her before he headed out. He didn't want to leave her, but he was expected on shift in twenty minutes.

Jason was in a foul mood. Leaving Carson was not what he wanted to do. But he couldn't find anyone to cover his shift – and leaving them shorthanded was not in his nature... even if his team understood.

"What the hell are you doing here?" Stoner barked out as Jason walked into the truck bay.

"Fuck off, Stoner. I couldn't leave the shift short."

"We could have managed. How's Carson?"

"Sad... angry... hell – her dick of an ex-husband wants her to sell the house. She found out yesterday."

"Wait – he asked her to sell the house, the day of the viewing? What an asshole."

"Yeah – he'd come to the house the night before... but her brother and I sent him away."

"Sent him away, huh?"

"Yep." Jason headed towards the bunk room, "I introduced him to my right fist though... so I don't think he will be bothering her again. At least, I hope not."

"That's my boy!" Stoner slapped him on the back. "The funeral tomorrow?"

"Yeah, Chief said I could go – so I'll head out for that, then come finish shift."

"Nah – you won't."

"What? I already had it approved."

"We talked to Chief. We are going as a department."

"What?? I don't expect you guys to do that... I can lose some hours and go on my own time."

"Jason," Chief's voice echoed through the bunk room, "Do you love this woman?"

Jason turned to eye his trusted mentor and Chief, "Of course I love her."

"Then she's part of this team too. We will all go, not just for you, but for her."

Jason's eyes welled with tears, he didn't know what to say. His whole team was going to support him and the woman he loved as she buried her son. Stoner wrapped his arm around Jason's shoulder, "You're our brother. We'd do this for any one of the guys on this team."

Jason nodded, unable to form a response. Stoner pulled his arm free, leaving Jason alone in the bunk room with the Chief. "Son," he sat down on an empty bed, "This woman has sparked life into your heart and I want to do whatever I can to keep it alive. She's been through something awful, but you – and this team can be here to help her through it. We have your back... and hers." He stood, pulling Jason into a hug. "You're like the son I never had – let us do this for you."

Jason only nodded, tears covering his face. Chief Donnelly was the man he hoped to be one day. "Thank you," he managed to get out. The sound of the alarm broke the awkward silence, reminding them they had a job to do. Jason hurried past the Chief towards his awaiting truck. While he never wanted anyone hurt, he prayed for a busy night – to keep his mind from worry.

The night blew by, leaving a few hours to sleep between calls – even though Jason didn't sleep. He couldn't keep his mind from Carson. The sun reminded him today was the day Carson's life would change forever. Even though she'd already said goodbye to Max – today would be the final farewell. He was pulling on his dress blues when the alarm sounded. Glaring at the clock on the wall, he cussed. The funeral was due to start in two hours. This call better be quick. He grabbed his dress jacket and hurried to the squad. Tossing the coat into the back, he climbed in.

"Don't worry – we'll get there in time." Jonesy tapped his arm, "I promise."

Jason simply nodded, closing his eyes as the truck pulled out from the bay. He didn't want to let her down – not today.

Carson stared at her reflection in the mirror. Today she would bury her son in the ground. She wasn't sure how to do it – how to say goodbye. Pulling her hair into a tight ponytail, she slipped into the black dress she'd worn yesterday. She didn't care if people frowned at her repeated attire. Hell, she didn't even want to go. Maybe she could stay home and pretend this was all a nightmare.

"Carson." Her brother's voice broke through her thoughts.

"In here."

Zeke pushed open the bathroom door, "You ready?"

Carson half smiled, taking in his appearance. He was in his Marine dress blues, his hat tucked under his arm, "Damn, Zeke. You look really good."

"Thanks, I just wish it was for a different reason."

"Me too... me too." Carson stepped into his hug, breathing in his aftershave. "Let's go get this over with."

"Have you heard from Jason?"

"No. He's probably busy."

"He'll be there, Carson."

"I know."

"He's a good man. I know you think it's too soon, but it's not. Phillip was never a good husband – you deserve someone who will love you through thick and thin. And Carson," Zeke gripped her shoulders, "Jason has been there in the worst moments of your life and not tucked tail. He loves you."

Carson smiled, "I know... but, Zeke," she looked at her feet, "I'm scared."

"That's fine, Carson. You're allowed to be scared – just don't run from it... him. Let him in, OK? I need to know you're going to be cared for when I leave today."

"Don't worry about me... I need you to be safe. Worrying about me will be a distraction you don't need."

"You're my sister... I'll never stop worrying about you," he tugged her hand,
"Now... let's go and say goodbye to Max."
Carson nodded and followed him out to
the car.

She stared at the hole that would soon
hold her son. She could hear the people
around her talking, their voices a murmur
inside her head, as they waited for the
minister to start the service.

"Carson," she heard someone to her
left speak, "I'm so sorry for your loss."
Glancing towards the voice, she was surprised to see the nurse who'd been at her
and Max's side the whole time he'd been
on life support.

"Thank you," was the only response
she could muster. The nurse, Carson
couldn't remember her name, nodded and
walked away.

Watching her walk away, she was taken
back to see Phillip standing against a tree.

Rage filled her blood. Storming towards him, "You fucking have some nerve."

"What the fuck are you going on about, Carson? He was my son too."

"You are such a phony. Leave, I don't want you here."

Phillip stepped into her space, his face inches from hers, "Fuck you. I will be here if I want to. What are you going to do? You're just a scared little girl."

"She might be scared, but I'm not." Jason's voice echoed through the cemetery.

"Oh – you want to hit me again? Go ahead – I'll have you arrested."

As Jason went to respond, a fist flew through the air, knocking Phillip to the ground. "Get this piece of shit out of here." Chief Donnelly spoke, pointing to a crumpled Phillip on the ground. "He can mourn his child, but not today – today is Carson's time to say goodbye."

Phillip pushed himself off the ground, "I'll have your badge." He pointed at the Chief.

"Son – everyone standing around here saw you threaten me." He glanced around at the men surrounding Jason and Carson.

Every member of Station 6 stood with their arms folded, including Zeke, who was menacing in his Marine uniform. They were all waiting for Phillip to move or speak.

"It's in your best interest to leave." Zeke warned him, "and if you try anything to hurt my sister – I have ways to dispose of a body and never get caught. Remember that, Phillip."

"Phillip," Diane approached him, grabbing his arm, "Let's just go."

Spitting on the ground, "Fine – I want to forget she ever existed anyway." They started towards the parking lot together.

"Oh, and Phillip," Carson called out, causing Phillip to turn, "I will be putting the house on the market this weekend. I'll contact the attorney Monday and let them know my intentions. You don't deserve it, but I want to start over – without your memory as well." She turned, wrapping her arm around Jason's bicep, "Let's go say goodbye to Max." Cutting her eyes towards Chief Donnelly, "Thank you, Chief."

"Carson – you're one of us now. We will always have your back."

Nodding, she tugged Jason towards the onlookers. They'd seen everything yet said nothing – it was as if they all knew Phillip was unworthy of this moment with Max.

24

Carson held onto Jason as though he was an anchor in turbulent seas. She listened as the minister spoke. He told stories of the little boy Max once was and how heaven was gaining a spirited young man. Carson let the tears flow down her cheeks as she stared at the casket that held her son. Jason tugged her into his side, reminding her that she was not alone. On her other side, stood her brother. The two men that would see her through this tragedy. The funeral had ended, but she stood, stock still. Jason and Zeke stayed by her side without a word. She knew they were giving her time to be ready. Time to leave her son.

"What am I going to do?" She mumbled into the wind, "Max – we were supposed to be a team. Remember? Team CarMax."

Jason held her tighter, Zeke rested his hand on her shoulder. "I don't know who I am without you. You were my world." She let the sob bubble up her gut, "I love you, little man. Say hi to grandma and grandpa." Turning she looked at her brother, "At least he will have them." He nodded, squeezing her arm.

"That he will." Zeke released her arm, "I have to go, Carson. I don't want to, but I have to report on base in an hour."

"I know. It's ok. I love you , Zeke. Stay safe over there." She tugged him into a hug, "You're all I have left."

"No, I'm not." He pushed her back to look in her eyes, "You have a good man, and a family that will support you." He nodded towards Jason, then towards the street beyond.

Turning, Carson smiled at Jason, then realized the station six's entire team stood, propped against their trucks. She couldn't believe they'd stayed – for her.

"They're his family – and he loves you, Carson. That means they're your family too." She nodded wordlessly and stepped into Jason's awaiting arms. He wrapped her up in an embrace, pressing his lips to her head.

"I know." She smiled, "Go on. I don't want you to get in trouble for being late. Thank you, Zeke."

"Don't thank me. I needed to be here. I loved that little boy too. I'll miss him just as much." Zeke swiped at the tear dripping down his face, "Take care of her, will ya?" He thrust his hand out, taking Jason's in his.

"I wouldn't have it any other way. Be safe out there."

Zeke nodded, hugging Carson one last time, before heading off towards the awaiting driver. He waved as they pulled from the curve.

"You ready to go home?"

"Don't you have to go back to work?"

"No. Chief told me to take the rest of the day off. It's only a few hours before end of shift anyway."

They walked hand in hand towards the firetruck and his crew.

"Chief," Carson reached out, intending to shake his hand. But he had other ideas and pulled her into a hug.

"I meant what I said earlier. You're family now. This man," he smiled towards Jason, "is like a son to me. You've given him back something he lost when his parents died. Lean on him when you need to, you hear me?" Carson nodded against the Chief's chest.

"Jason," Chief released Carson, "take this woman home and take good care of her. As of today, you're on leave, we'll see you in a couple of weeks." Chief clapped him on the shoulder and walked off. The rest of the crew hugged Carson and offered support.

Once the trucks pulled off, leaving Carson and Jason standing in the parking lot alone, she turned and smiled at him. "You have a great family, Jason."

"You do too – now."

She nodded, "Take me home."

Jason helped her into his truck and shut the door. She stared out into the cemetery, her eyes locked onto the spot that held her son. As Jason started to pull off, "Wait... please."

Jason stopped the truck, waiting for her to give him a signal it was ok to leave. Although her heart was breaking, she could feel the love radiating off Jason.

Slowly Jason eased the car forward, "You ready?"

She turned towards him, he could help heal the fractures left by Max's death.

He would be the one to show her love beyond tragedy.

Taking a deep breath, she gripped his hand in hers and nodded.

"I'm ready."

Epilogue

Jason watched as Carson flipped the sign to open. A lot had changed in the last year. She'd sold the house a week after Max's funeral and moved in with him into his house. She'd transformed his house into a home in a matter of weeks. It wasn't as big as her previous one, but it was big enough for them. Now, as he watched her open her bakery – he couldn't help but smile.

"What are you smiling at?" Carson walked towards him, wrapping her arms around his neck.

"You. I'm so damn proud of you, Carson." He pressed a kiss to her lips, "This place is amazing."

"Thanks... but it wouldn't have happened without your support. I owe you everything, Jason."

"You did this on your own, Car."

Carson glanced around the shop, smiling at her hard work. She'd decided to use her degree and skills to open her own bakery. And now... it was opening day. The door chimed, signaling a customer. Carson dropped her arms and turned to find Jason's entire station entering the shop.

"Where's my cupcakes?" Chief Donnelly smiled, pulling her into a bear hug.

"Right over there," Carson chuckled, "Pumpkin Spice just as you requested."

He pressed a kiss to her forehead, "Jason... you better hold onto this one tight – or I might steal her from you." He chuckled, tapping his belly as he walked towards the counter where his cupcakes awaited him.

Jason smiled at Carson. She was being hugged by every member of his fire-family. The sight made him warm all over.

"No need to worry, he's stuck with us." Carson's eyes twinkled with mischief.

"Us?" Jason blinked, "You telling me I have to compete with Chief?"

Carson walked towards him, "No..." She tugged his hand to her belly, "us."

Jason froze, his hand rested on her abdomen. He was trying to process what this meant. "Are you saying what I think you're saying?"

"Yes..." she bit her lip, "I'm pregnant."

"HOLY SHIT!" Stoner yelled out. Everyone started cheering, Jason just stood, staring at the woman he loved.

"Say something." Carson's eyebrows wrinkled with concern.

He glanced around at his team and grabbed her hand. Jason pulled her into the back, away from everyone's prying eyes.

"Are you sure? I mean – I didn't think you'd want any more kids."

"Well... I didn't think I would. Not after losing Max. But... I love you, Jason. And when I saw the positive sign on the test last month, I knew it was supposed to be this way. Max is gone, and I miss him every day. But he wouldn't want me to stop living. How about you? We've never talked about kids – hell, we aren't even married."

Jason knew, in this moment that this woman was his life. He would stop at nothing to protect her and show her happiness. He dropped to his knee, pulling the black box from his pocket. He'd planned on doing this later – after the opening of her bakery... but this was the moment.

"Jason," Carson gasped, her hands flying to her mouth.

"Carson. The day I answered the signal 41 – I had no idea how it would change my life. I didn't expect to find love out of a tragedy... but that's what I did. From the moment I met you, I knew you were the woman I wanted to be a hero for. You make me a better man. Will you do me the honor of becoming my wife?"

Carson dropped to her knees, "Yes..." she pressed her lips to his, "Yes... I'll be your wife." Jason slipped the ring onto her finger, tugging her into his arms as he did.

"I love you, Carson." He stood, pulling her to her feet, "and I love that we created a new life." He pressed his hands to her still flat belly.

Carson leaned into him, pressing her body against his, "I love you, Jason." She could feel him hardening beneath her.

"Shit – let's go outside before I take you here on your desk."

Carson giggled as he pulled her to the front of the bakery. Everyone was staring at them, waiting for one of them to speak.

Carson broke the silence, "We're getting married!" she thrust their entwined hands into the air, showing off her ring.

"And having a baby!" Jason hollered.

The crowd erupted into cheers! One by one everyone hugged and congratulated the happy couple. After what felt like an eternity, Carson pulled the door closed and locked it up. She and Jason stood on the sidewalk wrapped in each others arms. He pressed a kiss to her head, "You did it, Carson. Your bakery was a success."

"It was." She smiled at Jason, "Now, take me home so we can celebrate."

His lips quirked into a smile, "No need to ask twice." He herded her towards his truck and opened her door. Carson paused, glancing back towards her bakery.

"I love you, Max." she called out to the sky. As she got in and pulled the door closed, she looked towards the bakery one last time.

Max's glowed in the darkness, the sign lighting up the sky in an amber shade of red. Smiling she placed her hand on the life growing inside of her. She thought she lost everything the day Max died, but really, she'd found strength.

Strength to overcome the loss of her son.

Strength to start over and love again.

Turning towards Jason, "Let's go home."

The End

Signal 99: Freeing Felicity

<u>Felicity</u>

Felicity Jones has the worst luck in men. Ever since she walked away from her high school sweetheart, she's been in one bad relationship after another.

Now at twenty-eight, her current relationship has her rethinking life... She's pretty sure this guy is the worst of them all.

Left clinging to hope, Felicity prays there's someone out there who will free her from the monster she let in her bed.

Liam

Liam Carver has been with the department eleven years – on the SWAT team for six. He's seen his share of bullshit.

But this call out is different.

This time it's someone he knows.

Felicity broke his heart in high school when she went off to college and never looked back. He thought she was the one. Since then, he's sworn off relationships, saving himself from anymore heartache.

Seeing her brings up old feelings he thought he'd buried all those years ago.

Will a chance encounter be the thing that frees them both from the hurt that's held them prisoner all these years?

Or is it too late for Felicity to find redemption and chance at real love?

Find out in Signal 99: Freeing Felicity

Nerdy, Dirty, Inked, and Curvy, LC is Native to the Atlanta area and works as a Special Education Middle School Teacher. She is the proud mother/stepmother of 4 children – 2 boys and 2 girls. And, as if that wasn't enough chaos in the house, the family adopted 2 dogs. LC has been married for nearly two decades. Her husband is a huge supporter of her work and pushes her to excel at being a writer.

Follow her on:

Booksprout: LC Taylor
Twitter: AuthorLCTaylor
Facebook: AuthorLCTaylor
Instagram: AuthorLCTaylor

www.authorlctaylor.com

Made in the USA
Middletown, DE
04 February 2022